To the woman who had me at fifteen, thank you for showing me strength over becoming a statistic, for showing me how to love and embrace God, for always encouraging me to write, to FEEL and release. To my mother, thank you, I Love you, we made it.

PART ONE

"A bird doesn't sing because it has an answer, it sings because it has a song".

Maya Angelou

Chapter 1: Cara's Eye View

CARA

Cancer. The dreaded diagnosis no mother wants to hear. I turned slowly, and there they were, three pairs of eyes gawking back at me as I sat ass out in my hospital gown in disbelief. In my fifty-two years of life, I battled it all; three kids, the death of my husband, an ailing mother, an estranged father, and now I was about to brave the shit storm that is chemo.

A little about me: I'm Cara. I've always been resilient, fun-loving, and vibrant! At least that's the face I wanted the world to see. To see me as the best version of myself – even when I didn't feel like it.

I came from a massive family of ten brothers and sisters – five and five split right down the middle. I was the second to last girl in the *Brady Bunch* of ten, minus the father, huge home, and maid.

Our mother raised us on her own. However, she dabbled in her own fun and vitality as well. She often left me and my younger sister, Yolanda, in the care of our older siblings. My siblings and I were steeped heavily into our religion as devout Christians of Jehovah's truth. My mother dressed us every Sunday for the Kingdom Hall. We sat in the front row as she gleamed with pride.

I don't recall much about my upbringing besides my older sister leaving to go off and get married. My second oldest sister bossed us around with such an evil look in her eyes. Everyone else just fell in line with somewhat normal sibling behavior.

Mommy? Well, my mommy was always the center of attention – always smiling, laughing, and entertaining. Maybe that's where I got it. She dressed to the nines daily and kept us all alive and somewhat well. Her love always seemed like just enough, even though there were ten of us.

We moved from our hometown in Queens, NY, to a small town just north of Los Angelos when I was almost fifteen. Luckily, my older sister had already moved to the same area and had my nieces Mirabel and Tammy, who were twelve and seven. The family would be together again at last. We couldn't wait to get off the mean streets of New York and start over in sunny California.

Life was always easy for me. I just rolled with the punches and adjusted as I saw fit. I had no idea my life would take the twists and turns it did growing up, but alas, I made it out of my mother's home and into my husband's arms. I frequented places that my brothers and sisters wouldn't be caught dead. I loved raves, night hikes, and swimming pools. You know, all the stuff black folks "don't do." I did them anyway because that's where I found the most fun, the most safety and felt the most alive. That's also where I met Justin.

Justin swept me off my feet. His Caucasian background was an oversight to how he made me feel. His enthusiasm met my vitality, and together they danced in synchronicity. That's how it began, at least. He loved me. He showed me new things, exciting adventures, most of all, he made me feel joy. His smile always got me. His jokes kept me. He was the light of my evolving life, and I was his, until October 2002.

Back to the cancer. My world came crashing down. Internally I fell apart. Was it a death sentence? Was it an eye-opener to finally get my shit together regarding my health? Or was there more to this that I couldn't quite understand?

My kids. What was going to happen to my kids? My two oldest were in a position to care for themselves. Thank God one was working, and one was almost finished with high school.

My baby, Carli, was quieter than most fourteen-year olds. She struggled in school, and so desperately wanted to be like her older sisters. I battled with letting her be free and restricting her. I figured she was the baby and had been through a lot. I got it. So, I coddled her. She was quiet and watched a lot; she visually mapped out our routine – her sisters and me. She tried to get away with a lot using her sweet little face and soft voice that I'd become accustomed to weakening behind. I had to raise them alone the last nine years. We had found our sweet spot as of late, but now *this*. What was I going to do without them? I already felt them letting me go.

I spent the night in the hospital with my girls by my side. My local family of nieces, nephews, brothers, and sisters came to my bedside immediately. The calls came in, flowers sent, Facebook messages, and love. Everyone looked so desolate, so defeated, and so utterly lost. I kept them going with my jokes. Jokes were my thing.

To break the silence, I whispered, "Great, I finally lose all this weight, and this is what lemons I get in life? Gee, thanks!" I thought it was funny. It wasn't until I busted out laughing that everyone came to the present moment. They enjoyed seeing me smile. It hurt me just as much to see them laugh because I knew that my smile kept them going. At no point in this would I be allowed to be defeated, angry, and downright hurt.

So, I smiled. I smiled because it felt good to see them smile. To knew I had love and support from my eldest sister, my favorite nieces and great-nieces, and my growing nephew.

The hospital was beautiful. I was on the first floor which was, you guessed it, Oncology. My nurse was a beautiful Asian woman with the spirit of an angel. Janet. Oh, sweet Janet. She brought my family a sense of calm because, at this point, we knew nothing except that I came in with a fever and would be leaving with a prescription to die.

A knock came to the door. We all shouted in our family's loud nature, "COME IN!" The wave of laughter created a calm that felt so familiar.

A volunteer at the hospital, a young lady with brown hair and blue polo, brought her a piece of comfort. With just a chair and an acoustic guitar, she sang Michael Bublé's *Home*.

> *Another summer day is come and gone away*
> *In Paris and Rome, but I want to go home*
> *Mmmmmmmmmmmmm*
> *Maybe surrounded by a million people*
> *I still feel alone, I just want to go home*
> *Oh, I miss you, you know*
> *And I just feel like I'm living someone else's life*
> *It's like I just stepped outside*
> *When everything was going right*
> *And I know just why you could not come along with me*
> *That was not your dream, but you always believed in me*
> *Another winter day has come and gone away*
> *In either Paris or Rome, and I wanna go home*
> *Let me go home*

So apropos.

Chapter 2: Post Hospital

CARA

I overstayed my welcome at the hospital. So what! I'm dying. They can wait. Well, I didn't say that, but that's how I felt. I overstayed, but everyone was okay with it because our crazy family kept the floor lively.

Friends came to see me; *I comforted them*. My estranged brother came to see me; I comforted him as well. You get the point. There was a lot of sharing of old stories. There were tears of sadness and laughter. Man, was there laughter! People came to show their love to my little family, and all I could do was smile from ear to ear thanking my maker for such high spirits around me.

I lost a significant amount of weight in the last three months. There I was thinking that the infamous low carb diet was actually working. My hair touched my shoulders, and I was so proud to wear it out with a cute matching headband. I fit into jeans again! Can you believe it?! My fifteen years in leggings and expandable waistlines had finally come to an end.

Did I mention I had a man in my life? Maybe his presence had something to do with it. He encouraged and motivated me. He inspired me to change my lifestyle. You know, quit the stuff that kept me going for so long. So, I did because, for the first time since my deceased husband, I truly felt alive and didn't need any further assistance.

This new man loved me so much. A ghost of Christmas's past, he reappeared into my life after twenty or so years. Thanks to good ole Facebook. A friend of a friend turned lover; I guess you could say. Nonetheless, this man brought me back to life. He encouraged health and wellness. After much debate, I cut out dairy and *voila* my skin cleared up. He was my knight in shining armor.

The day finally came for me to leave the hospital. After two weeks of being pampered, looked after, and catered to, it was time for me to go home and fend for myself.

By this time, two teens and one impressionable pre-teen had taken over my small apartment. Their boyfriends had probably been there. I was sure underage drinking had commenced. God knew what else. But at that point, I didn't care.

My kids did their own thing — been that way since Dad died. In some irrational, bizarre, and invalidated reason, I felt guilty for his death. So, we co-parented. Crazy. I know. But it kept the peace, and I was able to do what I needed to do to stay sane.

I was discharged from the hospital with a bag of clothes and—according to the doctor— a bag of pain pills to keep me 'comfortable.'

I'm a recovering addict, sir; it's going to take another bag to make me 'comfortable.' I didn't say that. I just smiled.

I went to my mother's house, an even smaller apartment with thrift store finds turned treasures. She and one of my older brothers lived there. The cramped two-bedroom apartment had wall-to-wall stuff and barely any room to maneuver around. As beautiful and as crowded as everything was, somehow being with my mother made this world and this fight seem less chilling.

Maybe I didn't want to go home.

Being forced to look at the same crap I meant to dump a long time ago. To lay there and watch my daughters parent themselves and prepare for my untimely departure. I couldn't do it. The very thought of it made me sick. I had to be comfortable at this time. I had to have peace.

Everyone questioned why I wouldn't go home. The kids got tired of taking gas money off of my card and driving the short twenty-five-minute commute to see me. The burdens began. I understood their pain and let them cope as they saw fit. We had so much support right then that I was confident they were being looked out for. I just didn't have the energy.

The phone continued to ring off the hook with calls of support and people genuinely calling to see if my family and I needed anything. One afternoon, a special call came through that changed the course of my journey. I picked up the phone, and to my pleasant surprise, it was Mirabel.

"Hey, Cara. It's Mirabel just calling to say 'hi' and see how your doctor's appointment went?"

"Aww, Mirabel. You're always so caring. I'm doing okay. Mommy is probably ready for me to get out of her bed! Ha! Ha!" I said, smiling across the room, meeting eyes with my mother.

She laughed uncomfortably. "You are so silly. I'm so happy you're in good spirits. Why don't you try going home? I'll come and keep you company your first night."

"Mirabel, can I be honest? Going home is going to make me so depressed, just seeing everything there is just depressing and a reminder of my old life. Pre-cancer. I can't go there right now," I said, struggling to keep from feeling nothing but utter embarrassment.

"I figured that was the reason. So, Farrell and I were talking, and we have so many extra comforters and decorations, he decided we can to go to your house and fix your bed to make it higher, decorate your room and make it a peaceful place to come home to."

I fought back the tears.

"I would love that, Mirabel. That would be nice. Thank you. That's so thoughtful."

But that was her; Quick to throw in a helping hand. Mirabel was my eldest sister's eldest daughter. How'd she get so lucky to have such a sweetheart? We had a bond that we've shared for years. I taught her so much, and she the same for me. Our kids have been close since birth. She and her husband were my right hand for the longest, so for them to extend their heart in a gesture of this magnitude, I knew this niece of mine was something special.

So, I went home. Farrell and Mirabel did *exactly* what they said they would do. Farrell raised my bed higher for easier access to my walker. (I can't believe I'm using a walker and making it cute, might I add.) Mirabel brought fresh flowers and some lovely wall décor. She also cleaned and vacuumed. My great-niece wrote a welcome home note. My heart was bursting.

There I was at home in my new and improved living space. Looking around made me happy. My great-niece Tiffany made sure to have something pleasing to the eye in every corner I should so happen to look. She had that Capricorn way that we connected on; We liked things orderly and enjoyable. I was so blessed to have so many people on my team. I was confident of my fight ahead as the support was unreal.

Later that week, I finally got the results back to the type of cancer I had. Adenocarcinoma. Stomach cancer. The very thing I'd been trying to lose the last fifteen years came back with a vengeance. Ninety to ninety-five percent of stomach cancers are adenocarcinomas, aka cancer that forms deep within the lining of the stomach. Damn. Apparently, it was highly unavoidable. Nothing that I did or didn't do contributed to this, at least that's what I kept telling myself.

The ball was in motion; Doctors' scheduled me in for a laparoscopic biopsy, radiation, and chemo right after that. Way to get things lined up. Again the Capricorn way.

My appointment was set. But, I still had to battle with my insurance on why I deserved a fighting chance to live. They heard it all of the time, "but it is because of my three kids." The insurance claims adjuster promptly and forcefully explained to me in so many words that with low-income insurance, it's virtually impossible to get things moving at any faster rate. I failed to tell her I only had six months.

Now came the fun stuff. I had my surgery a month later and made it through successfully. Family flew in. The girls were looked after. Financial assistance was provided to help sustain our home while I fought the battle of *our* lifetime.

The surgery revealed it possibly started as cervical cancer. WHAT?! You mean to tell me I've been walking around with cancer in my body and never knew? Although I couldn't remember my last doctor's appointment, let alone physical. It was probably roughly thirteen years ago when my youngest was born, maybe. Unfortunately, and admittedly so I lived my life in the clouds, often numb to what life threw at me, cancer included.

It was time to draw up a living will that would eventually pass as the final article. *Ugh.* I wasn't ready, but I knew I had to get prepared at the same time. My nephew-in-law Farrell did that for a living. He dealt with finances and asset protection. He was set to come to my home and go over the most challenging decisions I've ever had to make. Not because I couldn't make them but because I know that I wouldn't be here to see them through. I knew my decision *directly* affected my daughters and the family as a whole. I wouldn't be here to know if it was a beneficial or damaging one. I sat there racking my brain and kicking myself for not letting him come to my home and set me up with some life insurance six years ago. He highlighted the dire need, especially after my husband died. "Noted but no thanks" was my response; That still wasn't enough to convince me.

Chapter 3: Brianna, Alana, and Carli

CARA

Brianna. She's the stronger of the two. She's the one who challenged my authority. The one who stepped up when I needed her. The one who quickly became my mirror after my many failed attempts at rehab.

Brianna loved family. She was close with Tiffany, my great-niece, daughter of Mirabel. I love their bond. She looked up to Tiffany like a big sister, which I adored. Tiffany was a great young lady to model. Mirabel did a fantastic job with her even though she, herself, was just a baby when she had Tiffany at fifteen.

Although twins, Brianna finished high school first. The girls eagerly convinced me to let them fail out of regular high school only to be accepted at the local charter school that was once labeled for the 'bad kids.' Fortunately, they enjoyed it enough to go daily and were actually mentioned in high honors by their teachers. Proud mom moment. Brianna now worked at a local sandwich shop and was making decent money for an eighteen-year-old fresh out of high school.

I met her eyes first after the doctor uttered the words that would forever change the course of everyone's life. I saw sadness. Fear mostly. After losing their father, I was all they had and now this. I thought she hated me, honestly. She was always so challenging with me. To see this pain on her angelic face, a face that looks a lot like mine, crushed me. My face, of course, before the self-inflicted damage to my skin, the distress to my liver that showed through the whites of my eyes, and my vibrancy. My vibrancy, my tenacity, and willpower all diminished over the years as I chased a feeling, a moment that would never come.

I love my Bri Bri. I shortened their names to cute pet names to keep them, my babies forever. Not sure if I'll get to see if it worked. I looked at each of them and wondered how I was going to brave face over these next few months trying to be a parent and friend at the same time.

I think she took it the hardest. However, she was the strongest of the three. So much like her damn dad. I guess I could be grateful that they've had such positive influences in their lives, even if I wasn't one of them.

The night we found out about the cancer, Brianna called Tiffany. She just sat on the phone and cried. The next thing I knew, in walked Tiffany, Mirabel, Tammy, my sister Sharon and more family. Wow. The first thing Mirabel said to me was, "We're here for you and the girls, Cara." And they were — every step of the way.

Alana. Baby B. My heart. She's the sweet twin. In so many words, she's the compassionate one, the caring one, and the one who often wore her heart on her sleeve. Sometimes a little too visible.

She's dating this guy that reminded me eerily of her father. It scared the crap out of me. He came from money. His family was extremely pleasant to my girls. They really stepped up financially at this time. But, his outbursts scared me. He was there for her at this time, so how could I argue that. They needed support too. Alana helped the most with Carli. I mean, she had to as she initially refused to get a job.

The minute we found out, she turned to Brianna, her strength. Then Carli turned to Alana. Eventually, we all lock eyes. One by one, a tear dropped from each eye in that room. Alana gets nervous in uncontrollable situations like these. Still, they held each other up, and for that, I was so proud.

Now that she finished high school, she was willing to get a job. Go figure. I think she finally understood that she might be on her own by the end of the year.

That night at the hospital, while the other two were sleeping, she came and laid with me. We held each other and cried. When I made a joke about how wet my hospital gown was, she made a joke about me being part of the hospital's wet t-shirt contest. We laughed a good laugh.

Jokes were our thing.

Carli, my baby of my three. I've babied her since her father's death. Again, the guilt. Her childhood was not like most. She saw things, heard things, and *felt* things that no growing child should. For that, I was so sorry. In the midst of finding my happiness, I allowed them to be submerged to a lifestyle they didn't deserve. But we did our best.

Carli was my baby. Thirteen years old, and she was true to her Gemini ways: Soft and gentle one moment and the next, visions of her father emerged and then back to sweet old Carli. She was the youngest and often fell in the shadows of the twins. You know the infamous intro "These are my kids: Alana, Brianna, *and* Carli" anything after the 'and' always got forgotten. At least that's what I assumed she felt.

I showered them with unnecessary things to fill a void I was unable to tend to. I was healing myself, and I did what I had to do. Carli slipped under my radar, and her grades drastically fell. It wasn't me, no, of course not, couldn't be. They wanted to put her on meds, said she was depressed, that's why she struggled so much. I mean, of course, that makes sense, she did watch her father kill himself.

Off to the pharmacy, we went.

The family was against me medicating her at such a young age. But she was *my* child, and I knew what was best.

Carli reacted a bit different to the cancer news. Stoic really. Her face went blank, and eyes disappeared under a wave of tears she struggled to keep in. She held her sisters' hands as they comforted her told her things would be okay. How were they so sure?

Carli knew the decision would have to be made. Somewhere deep down inside, she assumed she would just stay with her sisters, and they would live happily ever after without mom. In the days after the announcement to the family, Carli clung to me. For dear life, she hardly wanted to leave my side. She was afraid of a monster that her deceased father nor I could scare away.

This decision was going to be my hardest. If in the course on one year, give or take, I might be leaving this beautiful Earth, Carli's care and wellbeing would be the responsibility of someone else. I just had to decide who that would be.

I had nine brothers and sisters, and my mother was still alive. Should be easy, right? Wrong. Not everyone was willing. (Sad, I know.) And second, not everyone was mentally stable, let alone financially stable to take on the burden of raising a child in my honor. My sister Yolanda barely let me get my thoughts together before volunteering *not* to be considered due to her health and financial concerns. Understandable. My brothers and sisters just aren't that way, honestly. We laughed and joked around and stayed cordial for our ailing mother, but the closeness had been lacking for a while. That's why I sought adventure elsewhere. With countless nieces and nephews and extended family in neighboring states, the search continued. However, I already had my sights on someone special.

Chapter 4: October 2002

CARA

I met Justin in high school. Typical Jock. Typical Casanova. He swept me off my feet and kept me there. Having the twins later was a shock. Neither of us had twins in our family, at least not to our knowledge. That didn't stop our antics.

In high school, we would sneak off and get lost in the woods. He introduced me to drugs. To a way of life, nothing like my own. To a world that made me feel like the me, I was destined to be.

The drug use heavily fueled our dating life. It sat front row at our wedding. It was there to help me with post-partum after my girls were born. It was signed right into our marriage and would be the cause of our untimely parting.

We got high just for the hell of it. We got high with neighbors. We got high with my brother. We got high just to get high, and it was *amazing*.

I was always beautiful, but I became interesting when I was in the clouds. I could talk and talk and talk about any and every subject. I was often the life of many parties. It got to the point where I didn't want to be anything but high; Being a mom was easier that way. Hell, being his wife was easier that way too.

The takeoff was a blast, but the comedown was always a tumultuous wreck of emotions, anger, and coveting for more. Justin wasn't himself when he was high, but neither was I, so it worked. At least I thought it did.

He often went into these angry rages and used me as his punching bag. And I took it, and fought back like the New Yorker in me knew how to. My kids saw It all. The pushes into the wall turned to punches down my back. A bloody rage of hate spewed at me only to go in together and kiss our kids goodnight like the happy little couple we were. What a mess we called home.

We played the role perfectly. We took family pictures with our perfect girls showing our perfect lives. No one would have ever suspected.

One night we were at our place playing cards. The girls were at Mirabel's for the weekend. Justin got angry because he thought I cheated in our card game. I did not. He smacked me so hard. He had the look of the devil himself in his eyes. My brother just sat there, dumbfounded. Then he proceeded to shuffle the deck. They were best friends. Bros before hoes, I guess — no matter if it's your sister.

That's how things went up until the night of October 2002. We played the role well up until this point.

We moved into a beautiful penthouse apartment in an affluent neighborhood. Things seemed to be improving. The hits came less, and the family time increased. My heart was full. We hadn't gotten high in about two weeks. We both knew that if we did, we'd have to do it sparingly as the kids were getting up more in the middle of the night. Carli especially had night terrors.

It was about two weeks until Halloween and the girls hadn't decided on costumes. It was my bright idea to have a conversation with him just after one of his raging fits. We had gotten high that night, exorbitantly high. We argued about something that seems so irrelevant and hadn't spoken for about fifteen minutes. I brought up the costumes and what I liked the girls to wear. Three cute little Barbie dolls. I'd do their makeup, and it would be so adorable. Well, he didn't think so, and he went ballistic.

I don't recall much. Psychology says that it is very common to blackout during times of traumatic experience. I did just that. My husband shot me over Halloween costumes.

We argued back and forth for thirty-five minutes, and he was angry but manageable. Did I mention we were high?

8

His anger grew every five minutes. He went into our bedroom and rummaged for his gun lockbox, which wasn't locked because the last time he acted out, he went for it then too. Not worried at all, I stared at him, our king size bed separating us. The bed felt like an ocean and puddle all at the same time.

"What are you going to do, Justin? Shoot me? Shoot me over some costumes?"

BANG.

My greatest nightmare. The love of my life shot me. In the chest. In our home. As I fell to the floor, time seemed to stop on the way down. Now upside down, I saw my three heartbeats scared out of their minds. Nothing, not even Mom, could protect them for what was to come next.

"OH MY GOD, CARA!" he cried.

BANG.

Justin shot himself. Point blank in the temple of his head. Pink parts and matter spattered on my freshly painted walls as I lay there, floating in and out of consciousness. My children's screeching cries kept me coming to. Meanwhile, the shock of it all helped me drift away.

Neighbors called the police, and I was carted off to the nearest hospital. My high-rise apartment was now a crime scene — a murder scene, excuse me. He was still alive when I was finally able to see him at the hospital. Social workers were involved because of the kids in the home. They knew we were high out of our minds. They knew he did this in front of them. They knew I was not fit to mother any longer.

When I was able to see him, I cried. I cried because I loved him. Because I loved us. He was it for me despite what we did with our time together. I made the choice to pull the plug, but to never let him go.

He shot me on the left side of my chest. The bullet went through my left breast and out the back, just missing a few main arteries that could've killed me instantly. Thank God I was alive. I truly felt that hearing him scream, "Oh My God, Cara" was regret. Maybe he thought he killed me and couldn't live without me. But then you leave our kids without *any* parents?

I blamed myself for his death for many years after. If I hadn't brought up the costumes. If I hadn't agreed to get high after being clean for two weeks. If I hadn't allowed a gun into our home when I knew drug abuse was our thing.

I went to counseling. I made the girls go too. We did it as a family. Again, the guilt reared its ugly head. That's when things shifted in the parent-child relationship. That guilt of his passing weighed on my heart so heavy that I just let the girls do whatever. They mouthed off. I took it. They snuck out. I caught them but hardly kept them on punishment.

My sister saw them on social media in a way not pleasing to most parents. I went off on her and told her to mind her business. These were my kids, and no one was going to take them from me.

Although that was almost the case when toxicology reports came back. Considering the nature of the crime scene and the fact that children were present, this had CPS written all over it. My second worst nightmare; I was at risk of losing my kids.

The night of the shooting, the girls stayed at a neighbor's until my brother could pick them up. From there, they cramped into my mother's queen-sized bed. That night, in her tiny apartment, she prayed over them. She prayed for the soul of my deceased husband and me, her daughter in need.

When the news broke to the family, everyone was distraught but okay considering. They were just happy I was alive. The girls then went to Mirabel and Farrell's home, which was about thirty minutes north.

Talks had already started circulating that I was losing the girls. First in line, before anything could be said, Mirabel and Farrell volunteered their home. They offred to take in all three of my kids. They were willing to take on my three responsibilities in addition to their own three kids — all while trying to establish themselves as well. That spoke volumes to me and everyone in the family. Again, such special people.

Chapter 5: Mirabel

CARA

Mirabel was my oldest sister, Sharon's daughter. The gatekeeper of all secrets and the center of all love. I say this to say that my young niece had seen it all. She managed to watch every single person's destruction. Destruction that seemed to come with the family name. Destruction that never seemed to touch her. It only motivated her to do better and be free from the mental turmoil we all seemed to carry with us.

She's my oldest niece, and coincidentally enough, we look very similar. Our full cheeks always gave us away.

Anyways, Mirabel, my older sister Yolanda and I were three peas in a pod when we got to California. We were all close as teens, but eventually, I went off and got married, and the dynamics changed. Mirabel and I remained close over the years and into adulthood while Yolanda moved up north with her two daughters. I was a married woman with a growing family. Mirabel had her daughter Tiffany. Our kids were close, and new family dynamics were birthed.

We did holidays every so often at Mirabel's. She was the only one with a home big enough and warm enough to house all the crazy in the family. Our kids were close. I was so proud that my girls had a cousin to look after them and guide them and teach those things only a cousin should.

I've always been proud of my niece and nephew-in-law. You could say I was slightly envious, but I never let that envy turn into hate for them. It was pure admiration at this point. I liked to think that she looked up to me. That, at one point, my model for taking care of a man and family was one she admired. Even though things unfolded the way they did, my intentions had always been love.

When I initially found out about the cancer, she was one of the first calls I made. I needed strength, and she was it. To meet her gaze upon their arrival at the hospital was a moment I never forgot. I could see the pain in her spirit that her favorite aunt and chosen friend might not be here much longer. The sting in her face nearly crippled me. I quickly tossed a joke out. Through streaming tears, she laughed, and I found my strength.

During one of the many nights in the hospital, I called Mirabel. My fifth call to her that day. She didn't care one bit because she afforded herself the opportunity to work from home.

The most fulfilling work, she started her own business running a daycare! Makes sense even as a mother at a young age she's always had a knack for children — hell, for family. That mothering nature was something the rest of us drastically lacked.

When she answered the phone for the fifth time, she didn't sound bothered; she actually seemed excited to hear from me *again*. I guess I didn't want to be alone with my thoughts. To face the harsh reality that I was literally living to die. I had all the time in the world (for now) and a free phone line, so I called any and everyone I could to keep me from myself.

I expressed to her that I was faced with a tough decision in regards to Carli's care. I told her that my sister Yolanda who lived upstate, shut me down immediately before I could even ask. Yes, she had health issues. Yes, diabetes is a very real disease. However, I was *really* losing my *life*, and my own sister took herself out of this deathly equation. My twin girls, just eighteen years old, didn't want the responsibility of being parents, grieving, *and* trying to make something of themselves. My only desire was that my girls stayed together or as close together as possible.

We spoke about this very real matter. The thing I loved about Mirabel was her ability to think clearly, logically, and fair. She assured me that whatever my decision was, I'd be fully supported on all avenues. That was her, quick to find a solution and even quicker to lend a helping hand.

"I'm scared, Mirabel. Terrified. I talked to the girls, and they don't want the responsibility of raising Carli."

She paused and proceeded with caution. "I know you're scared, and you know we support you in whatever and whoever you decide. Just let me know so we can get things in writing."

"Mirabel, do you know I'm dying?" eager to get the elephant out of the room.

"Oh, Cara. I do, and I promise the kids are going to be alright. I'll see to it myself."

And we sat in the most comfortable stillness I'd felt in a long time.

Chapter 6: Farrell

CARA

Farrell had been around for as long as I could remember. Mirabel and him met as young adults and had genuinely grown through life together. Justin respected him. I adored him and what he became to my family. My girls loved their bonus cousin.

Gosh, when I think about it, theirs was the last wedding my family and I attended as a unit. Wow, really puts life into perspective. We danced at their wedding. They sobbed at his funeral. Soon they would be crying at mine.

Anyways, back to Farrell. He was a man with quiet confidence and strength. A Capricorn himself, we instantly had a connection. I took him in as my family because he had always been so good to mine. He was respected in the family. To be honest, he was really the only male figure who was around consistently. He excelled in business and was the ultimate family man, father, and friend.

His office was in the same area of the hospital, and he would often stop in to see how things were, to see if I needed anything, or to chat.

He was present when I met with the initial social worker assigned to my death — I mean case. He was there to go over my will before my surgery. Thank goodness he was there because I tried to joke my way through it and quickly saw how dead the crowd was.

"It's ok, Cara. We can go over the rest of this later. I can sit with you and explain everything when you're home."

"Thank you, Farrell. This is all so crazy, but I want to sincerely thank you for being such a great man to my niece and the family. You have been there for *everyone* and support your wife through it all too. She's so lucky to have you, Farrell. Seriously, I just want to say *'thank you'* from the bottom of my heart."

Reaching for my hand, "Cara, it's no problem. That's what family is for; You show up, you be there, and lend support. So, *thank you* for trusting me."

"Such a Capricorn thing to say!"

We laughed together and nodded in agreement.

I enjoyed seeing Mirabel and Farrell together. It was pleasing to know that my niece, who often looked up to me, married an amazing man and was living her life on her own terms. It made me so proud to bear witness to the power of black love.

Farrell was a successful businessman. Finances. Something we all needed assistance with. Yes, I'm still kicking myself for not letting him come to set me up with life Insurance, but there we were. I was just elated to know he was willing and able to help with this end of life stuff because I wasn't quite prepared.

The home they created for themselves was the hub for the family. Family parties, get-togethers, Sunday dinners, any and everything took place at their home. They were always so inviting. Farrell was a great father. Not only did he raise my great-niece, who was not his biologically, but he was also an amazing father to his daughter and the son he shared with my niece. It was a breath of fresh air to know my girls had a positive male influence in their life. Someone they respected, loved, and appreciated highly — especially after their father died.

We sat at my kitchen table in the morning. I finally agreed to let him come and set my end of life wishes. He came in doting a binder given to me by the hospital's social worker. I asked if he could sift through it and help me make sense of all of it.

"Ok, I looked through the binder. A Lot of this information doesn't apply to you as you don't possess assets such as a home or business. We just need to fine-tune what you'd like done with Carli and..."

We both paused. Toggling from businessman to nephew, I could see his Adam's apple quivering. His voice cracked slightly as he muttered the last few words, "Funeral wishes."

And there I lost it. Every ounce of strength I'd carried with me fizzled quickly away. Every joke I had in me, jokes that I knew would take me to my final resting place, were now jokes that couldn't find their way up passed the lump in my throat. At that moment, everything froze, and the only liquid assets I could release at that tender moment were the ones that came directly from my eyes.

He came over to hug me. He took his business cap off and became my loving nephew. We sat in my dining room, just us two with my husband's funeral portrait surveying over us. Justin's bold smile and mysterious eyes showed me precisely who his choice was, and I couldn't agree more.

Chapter 7: Decision

<u>CARA</u>

In third party transfer of parental responsibility, there are many areas to consider. I had been back and forth with each one of them, and here's what I came up with:

The best interest of the child must be considered. Rightfully so. Carli had spent a lot of time at the Davis' home and loved hanging with their youngest son, Drew. Check.

Next, I had to consider the wishes of the child. Carli expressed she would love to be with her sisters but understood that this might not be best. When presented with the idea of Mirabel, a calm came over her, and she was all in. Check.

Then we had the child's relationship with the third party. Easy. Carli loved her cousins and was comfortable around them. Although we understood the dynamics might change from cousin to parent, I was still confident that the relationship and the love wouldn't change. Check.

Lastly, the child's lifestyle adjustment to school, home, and community needed to be highlighted. Mirabel lived about thirty minutes from our apartment, so Carli would still have access to her sisters, which is not something that is up for debate at this time. I wanted my girls to be together to continue to have that sister bond even if I was not there to see to it. I still wanted my girls to have access to their little sister, and a thirty-minute commute was nothing. As far as school went, Carli had fallen severely behind. In efforts to preserve our time together, I pulled her out and allowed her to do homeschool. She'd been through a lot in her short life, and since my diagnosis, her focus had been off. Hell, the same, was true for all of us as our family routine and dynamics were nonexistent. The only agenda now for all of us was just to survive. Check.

Next, we had to prove the non-parents' ability to provide for the child financially and emotionally. Mirabel and Farrell had a big enough home to house her. More importantly, they loved my kids so much that they had always treated them like their own. I knew she'd be happy to come out from under the shadow of the twins. She would get a real chance at a real family, and the idea of it all excited my dying spirit. Check.

And finally, the length of time the child had spent in a stable, loving home. I wanted to think I created a loving home from my girls. I knew I did. However, the stability had been lacking as of late. The stability was lacking from the beginning of it all honestly. We were never fully stable as a family, so this aspect I couldn't comment too deeply about because I also don't know what a stable *and* loving home looked like. So, it was my last wish to give my children what I did not have. My youngest child would to get a chance to experience a healthy existence. I'd finally provide her with something that couldn't be taken away, a life of *peace*.

In my small apartment on that cold winter day, I made the final decision to relinquish my parental responsibilities to that of my niece and nephew, Mirabel and Farrell Davis.

Chapter 8: Revelations 21:4

CARA

"911, what's your emergency?"
As she dialed her sister's number from the landline, faint screams in the background caused Tammy to struggle to hear the operator.
"Mom is throwing up! I don't know what is going on. I called the ambulance for her. Her arm is waving wildly in the air. I don't know what to do!"
Mirabel held tight to a deepened exhale within her. She sat there in silence, praying hard within her subconscious. She slowly dialed her daughter's cell only to be greeted with her cheery voicemail repeatedly. "Hey, hey. You've reached —" Click.
She dialed again. This time, her fingers moved independently of her mind.
"Hey, hey —" Click.
Frustrated and anxious, Mirabel shouted upstairs for her sleeping husband. Tiny hands and feet came trickling into her home daycare, ready for what they expected to be another fun-filled day with Ms. Mirabel.
Tammy, still frantic on the phone with the 911 operator, began to tell her the events of the morning.
"No, she didn't sleep much last night."
"I'm not sure."
Sharon faded in and out of consciousness. She looked to Tammy with a look of despair in her eyes. Tammy, the youngest, and Sharon shared her a tiny two-bedroom apartment that was located down the street from Mirabel. The apartment suddenly felt vast and foreign.
While on the phone with the operator, Tammy grabbed a few essential items to take to the hospital. She shoved the sadness down deep within her as she packed Mom's bag with uncertainty filing its brim.
"She just started throwing up as I was getting ready for work and complained of her right arm hurting..."
"Ma'am, I've called the ambulance. They should be there shortly." The operator phoned in dispatch, "We have an African American female. Sixty years old. Possible cardiac arrest."
And just like that, Tammy's ears fell deaf, and she dropped the phone as first responders rushed passed her to revive her ailing mother. Then they all went off to the local hospital.
Back at Mirabel's home, the children played quietly while the phone rang off the hook. Mirabel, who is unable to focus fully and unable to reach her daughter, began calling her daycare parents to notify them of a pending family emergency.
Tiffany awoke from a drunken night of irresponsibility to her phone vibrating under her pillow. As she attempted to accept the call, her phone died.
She'd spent the night at a friend's and slept right through the eight calls from home.
What the hell happened?!
Tiffany jumped up, rushing out of her drunken slumber. As she peered out the window, she noticed birds chirping and the sun peeking over the fence in what looked to be a beautiful day ahead. Tiffany gathered her items and hurried out the door into her car to charge her phone. She called her mom as she zoomed up the highway, not knowing what to expect when she arrived.
"Hey, Mom —"
"Why didn't you answer your phone?!" interrupted Mirabel.
"I was sleep! What's going on?" Both of them frantic. Both unable to fully uncover the very real elephant in the car, in the room, on the phone.
What the hell happened?!

"They rushed Grandma to the hospital." Silence ensued.

"I'm on the way."

They both hung up and sent up the same prayers.

Speeding up the highway, Tiffany began to draw inward. How could she be so stupid to be in a drunken slumber as her precious granny was being rushed to the hospital? A thought flashed into her head. Granny had left her a voicemail a few days ago, but she hadn't had time to return her call or stop by.

"Hey, Sweet Pea. It's Grandma. I made you some ribs. I know they are your favorite. Let me know if you can stop by. Remember, Grandma loves you. Don't forget me."

And the tears fell uncontrollably, unmasked, and ugly. The tears fell because Tiffany knew deep down what she might not have wanted to admit at the time. And so the tears continued to fall.

What the hell happened?!

By the time she made her way home, Tiffany had managed to dry her eyes and look somewhat presentable. She could show up and be a rock for her mother.

Mirabel opened the door, and the look on her face was unforgettable. Her mother's face was frantic. It was the face of a mother unsure of how to live without her own mother. It was a face full of fears hidden by the tears that continued to fall. They embraced one another. As the last of the daycare children left, Mirabel, Farrell, and Tiffany made their way to the local hospital where they would meet Tammy and await their fate.

Tiffany made calls to work while grabbing a cup of coffee to awaken her own dying spirit somewhat. *Ugh, must give up vodka.* She phoned work to let her boss and staff know that there was a pending emergency with family, and she wasn't sure if and when she'd be in.

At the hospital, they made their way to the fourth floor, Cardiac unit. Nurses flashed by. Doctors answered pages. They stood there, unaware of what those elevator doors would reveal.

They sat in the family waiting room, quietly updating family members and responding to texts. They were so unnecessarily busy to keep from the pending thoughts of doom ahead.

Dr. Jeffries was the presiding doctor that morning. He approached the family with eagerness and delivered the news many hoped would be positive.

"Your mom is a very sick lady. She had a massive heart attack. Her heart is only working at about twenty percent on its own right now. We put in a stent; however, it's only a temporary fix. With her being a Jehovah's Witness and not taking blood, our options are limited. We have her sedated right now, and you can see her once we move her to ICU, which should be within the hour."

As the news penetrated each eardrum in that small space, the weakening of knees soon followed. Tiffany watched her mother go weak as Farrell attempted to hold her up. Tammy fell into Aunt Sally as she tried to walk away, only finding stability and comfort against a wall. Tiffany walked away. Stark in her spirit, she walked towards an abandoned corner and let out her fears and tears. Her wail seemed to instinctively break her own heart right there in the Cardiac unit, go figure.

Back in the family waiting room, Mirabel, Tammy, Tiffany, and Farrell sat waiting. Everything was uncomfortably still. The news on in the background, nurses and hospital personnel rushed by as the elevator opened, and what they all saw could never be forgotten.

Sharon's body nearly lifeless strapped to the hospital bed. A protruding belly and IV lines tracing the perimeter of her sweet face. Beeps and buzzing of heart monitors disrupted the silence in their hearts. In and out her inhale and exhale assisted, tubes running down her throat, eyes closed seemingly dreaming of a better day.

The family watched their mother and grandmother be carted away up to ICU, where they would soon follow. All of them sat in stillness as the sting of being in the hospital for a loved one continued to pierce.

"Here. Tiffany, you need to eat something." Mirabel said while handing Tiffany a pack of vending machine graham crackers.

"No thanks, Mom. You go ahead and eat it." Tiffany, pushed the graham crackers back towards her mother.

"No! You need to eat something. *Here!*" Mirabel shoved it back to Tiffany, as she held a lost look of a mother trying to comfort her daughter when she needed comforting herself.

"MOM, I DON'T WANT IT!!!" and everyone in the family waiting room started laughing. Laughter was our thing, and Tiffany smiled at her mother with content.

It was nothing but a mother feeling helpless in her role as a daughter. The only way to combat that was for her to feed and console her own. Here's the thing, the laughter is what satisfied Tiffany's soul the most. It had nothing to do with that stale graham cracker. Laughter in her family was familiar, it was comforting and meant that no matter what, we would see *this* through and keep our spirits light as we go, at least that's what she thought.

Approaching the family, now in full cackle and banter, Dr. Jeffries and his nurse came into the waiting room. They gave the family the green light to see Sharon.

As they transported her up to ICU, the pain of what they were witnessing started to set in. Dr. Jeffries made it clear that she probably should have died during that attack, another sunken feeling of defeat. As she arrived in ICU, the family followed suit forming a line of love to see their ailing mother and grandmother. Her eyes flickered open and closed, and she tried to make sense of her new view. Unable to fully speak, a teardrop formed at the corner of her eye and like a worn levy gave way to her sadness. Scared and unaware of what was coming next, Sharon closed her eyes and prayed to her God. The family filed in attempting to display a strength they *only* got from her.

Through all the excitement and sedation, Sharon found the strength to speak to her loved ones. "Make sure they know I am a Witness and don't take blood." Holding Tammy's hand, Tammy and Mirabel reassured her that it's in her chart, and everyone working on her case will be made aware.

"I had a heart attack? They said I had a heart attack? I — I just can't believe it." Sharon whispered in complete disbelief and shock.

Mirabel stroked her hair, "You did, Mom. Dr. Jeffries is going to take great care of you. In the meantime, try to rest. We'll come and check on you tonight. Aunt Sally is talking to the nurses to make sure they are aware of your case. Don't worry. You're in good hands, Mom."

Sharon drifted off to sleep. The family filed out of the room and back into the waiting room, where they dried their eyes and prepared for whatever was coming next.

That night Sharon slept somewhat peacefully as the beeps and buzzing persisted and penetrated even in her dreams. That night she dreamt of the new system. A faint smile quivered on her lips as she dreamed of green grasses, feeding the elephants, living amongst the land, no pain, no sadness, and pure tranquility. She drifted off to sleep, reciting the lines silently to one of her most teachable scriptures. Revelations, the power of God's will, was seen there through passages emphasizing his beautiful work. For the first time in weeks, she was able to sleep peacefully.

"He will wipe every tear from their eyes. There will be no more death' or pain, for the old order of things has passed away. Revelations 21:4."

A month had passed since Sharon's initial attack. I, on the other hand, had made great strides with the chemotherapy rounds. My hair was completely gone; Bald as an eagle. I didn't mind because my nieces and daughters continued to make me feel beautiful as I went through this process of unveiling. One of my nieces did those fancy eyelash extensions once when I was hospitalized a few weeks ago. Gosh, I felt so beautiful that day! I wore a wig from time to time; A short one with a bang that fed into my sunken cheeks. I walked with a walker now. Since the cancer had metastasized to my bones, I had to have rods placed in both femurs to prevent a total break of the hip. So I'd gotten really acquainted with said walker. I visited Sharon when I was able to; When my levels were at a decent range to tolerate the germ-infested walls of the Intensive Care Unit. Go figure, and I thought I would find myself here for an extended stay rather than visiting my eldest sister with our mother in tow.

Another week went by. The doctors were now at the point of removing the balloon that was inserted into Sharon's heart. They explained to the family that for someone as sick as my big sister, this was a temporary fix in preparation for open-heart surgery. Because she was a Witness and couldn't take blood, the options were severely limited. They were running out of time. They explained that once the balloon is removed, there was a high chance of her passing shortly after.

Moments before her surgery, the family filed in one by one meeting Sharon at her bedside with warm smiles and aching hearts to send their love and well wishes. She laughed and joked as if she were in the hospital for a routine checkup and not to check out ultimately. Elders from her congregation made their way to read their scriptures. They facilitated Sharon in finding a level of peace that could only be brought on by none other than the Holy Spirit.

Mirabel, Tammy, and Tiffany entered her room shortly before she was carted off and prayed with her. Unsure of what was next, each of them took what they could from the moment. They tried to be as strong as possible for her.

Her hands quivered in fear, a fear she hid from the rest of her visitors. Sharon spoke to her girls, "This might be it for me, ladies. If anything, I really want you to get to know Jehovah, our God."

Mirabel's eyes met Tiffany's and Tiffany's to Tammy and back to Sharon as she worked to hide the affliction on her face while fidgeting with her signature red nails. "He's done some beautiful things. I want you guys to know all about him and his amazing works. I want to see you in the new system. I gotta have my girls with me in the new system." She smiled, fighting back the tears.

That was the first time since her initial heart attack that the three of them felt the panic in her already breaking heart. Tears fell from each of their eyes. She quickly instructed them not to cry, be strong, and be like she raised them to be — fearless in the face of adversity because God was on their side. And like she always told them, "I didn't raise no weak women."

Everyone waited patiently for the procedure to commence. The surgeon gave notice that her heart could possibly give way in the next days. Sharon continued to laugh and joke and was extremely vocal with nurses and hospital staff just minutes after the surgery. A medical marvel yet again. With a heart working at only fifteen to twenty percent, Sharon was supposed to be in critical condition, unable to speak, let alone laugh and joke.

Growing a little more stir crazy as the hours passed, Sharon was adamant about getting someone to smuggle food onto the ICU floor. She phoned Tiffany and requested a Slurpee. Tiffany declined. Sharon called Mirabel, but before she could even get her request out, Mirabel informed her that she was unable to bring her any food. Sharon, with an attitude, hung up the phone.

Sharon then phoned her son-in-law Farrell. She was sure he would do it. He always went above and beyond for everyone in the family, so she called him and put her request in for a Dairy Queen ice cream sundae with sprinkles and whipped cream. "I'm sorry, Mom. I can't do that. You know the situation. I'm sorry, Mom."

CLICK. That was Sharon; She wanted what she wanted when she wanted. Unfortunately, this was not a fight she would win with her family.

Sharon's prognosis worsened after getting the report from her surgeon about the state of her aching heart. Arrangements were made to move her to hospice care (up a few floors in the hospital) until the family could decide what was next. As the chosen ones to make the final decisions, Tammy and Aunt Sally agreed on a charming hospice home not too far from the hospital. Sharon would go there in a few days when a bed was available.

The family then decided that they would allow Sharon to have what would become her last meal. Her request: lobster tail and an ice cream sundae. The family obliged, and Sharon had a last meal of her favorite comfort foods as hospice arrangements were being made.

Mirabel's birthday was fast approaching, and she had plans to have a big fortieth birthday bash. However, given the circumstances, she was unable to get into the birthday spirit fully.

Friends and family came together to celebrate her while silently wondering if these would, in fact, be Sharon's last days. Family arrived for a night of fun at the Davis home. They hosted a pajama jammy jam to bring everyone together to laugh a little and enjoy these quick moments of respite from dealing with doctors, nurses, phone calls, etc.

Everyone just needed a break, and I, for one, needed to just see my family in good spirits again. We got together for a family game night and pot luck. Everyone came dressed in their favorite jammies. We played games, laughed, ate way too much, and for a moment, let the sadness slip away.

We played the Wii game, Michael Jackson I think it was. I watched my girls, my nieces, and nephews let loose in a fashion that had been prevented given the recent lemons life so graciously provided.

The next morning, bright and early, Mirabel was frightened out of her sleep from a phone call from the hospital. This time it was from Sharon's hospital room.

"Hello, Mom. Is everything okay?"

"I'm scared, Mirabel." Her voice was drowned out by the constant beeps and buzzing of her monitors.

"I know, Mom. But, you're going to be okay. You're going to be transported to the hospice house later this evening, and we'll come down to get you set up and situated so you are comfortable, okay?"

"Okay. I'm terrified, Mirabel. Please come down here soon."

"Okay, Mom. We'll be down soon."

Mirabel hung up the phone and prayed. This entire time she was only able to hold herself together because of her mother's strength and tenacity. Today she heard something different in the quiver of her voice. Mirabel's mother was approaching the end of her life. Sharon was frightened to the point of needing to hear her eldest daughter's voice for reassurance.

That evening Sharon was transported via medical transfer to the hospice home where she would be made comfortable. It was a cozy home in a lovely quaint neighborhood not too far from the beach. Sharon's hospice home was one just like any other home with four bedrooms. Each room was equipped with a hospital bed, small sofa, television unit, and a window or sliding glass door.

The home smelled of lavender and lemongrass; Calming and suitable aromas to satisfy the nerves of those entering and ultimately exiting. There was a kitchen where home-cooked meals were prepared and a common area with artworks of serene landscapes. It was a beautiful home with a staff that prided themselves on exceptional bedside manner and a level of compassion comparable to angels themselves.

The family arrived in the late afternoon. By this time, Sharon was unresponsive and nearly comatose. The family was told she was aggressive, slightly insulting, and combative upon transfer. So, she was administered Ativan to 'relax' her during her transition into the hospice home, and well, you know the rest.

"Wow, this place is really nice. I am so glad we decided on this rather than bringing her home. That would've been way too difficult to handle." Mirabel said as she walked through the room, making sure things were in tip-top shape for her mother.

"I wish she could see it. She would be so happy to be out of that hospital finally!" Tiffany said, followed by a nervous laugh. Tiffany had already decided she was going to spend that evening with her beloved grandma. She'd vowed to stay as long as possible to make sure she was comfortable in the days to follow.

It was the evening of May 22. Tiffany made herself comfortable on the small sofa, which was situated just to the left of the hospital bed. Her grandmother lay in peaceful slumber in her favorite nightgown and pink bonnet. They spent the evening scrolling the TV as Tiffany continued to speak to her in standard nature. As the sun began to set, Tiffany went into her duffle bag where she'd packed her Nikon camera, Johnson's baby lotion, and her journal for the evening. Sharon loved Johnson's baby lotion even at sixty years old. That was her go-to after shower moisturizer. Tiffany brought her journal to capture her emotions as they spent this time together. She brought her camera to capture what could be her last photos. Everything became so surreal.

Tiffany pulled back the blanket to her grandmother's hospital bed and revealed her weeping extremities. She pulled out the pink Johnsons baby lotion and squeezed a dime-sized amount into her hands. She began to effleurage up her grandmother's calves, around her knee, circling down around the ankle. She made swift strokes around the feet, through her toes that were painted the color of love. Tiffany massaged her way up to her arms and poured her way up, circling her grandmother's elbow. She noticed the moisture in her skin, its elasticity, and luster. She continued to massage past the veins of her arm and beyond the bend in her flesh. She softly pushed her way up to her shoulder and spilled on to her chest and back down, dividing amongst her fingers. She gently caressed each finger, studying her nails in their natural state, painted red with joy, long and beautiful. She worked her way across her chest, making peace with the gold chains around her neck. The simple gold chain was the second half of a best friend necklace. She began to sing. She sang a song that came so natural, one that she never sang before but felt compelled to sing it to her grandmother in her passing days, one that she once sang to her as a little girl.

> Summertime and the livin' is easy,
> Fish are jumpin' and the cotton is high,
> Oh, your daddy is rich and your ma is good lookin',
> So hush little baby don't you cry.

Sharon opened her eyes almost as if to say a quick 'thank you. I love you' to Tiffany. Then, she closed her eyes and drifted off to sleep. Tiffany continued to sing and massage her favorite lotion into her skin.

The hours passed, and the day transitioned into dusk. Sharon continued her slumber as Tiffany watched her intently praying, finding peace, and reminiscing on their lives together.

Early the next morning, nurses and hospice staff came in. They asked Tiffany to step out while they cleaned and changed Sharon. At this time, her breathing was slightly labored yet productive; however, she was still unresponsive. Tiffany stepped out of the room as her phone rang.

"Hey, Mom."

"Hey, babe. How are you? How's she doing?"

"She opened her eyes briefly for me. I don't think she was really there, *there*, but it was nice!" Mirabel could hear the tears swelling up behind her smile.

"The nurses called late last night and said that she is actively transitioning and they don't want you there alone. Why don't you come home and we'll go back together this afternoon?"

"No, I'm not leaving her alone." Tiffany growing in frustration, paced the living room area of the hospice home.

"Come on, babe. Do this for me. I don't want you there alone, either. Besides, Tammy is going down there soon so she won't be alone. Come on, babe."

"Tammy is coming?"

"Yes."

"Okay, fine. I'll go into work for a bit and leave around twelve and meet her down there."

"Okay, sounds good. I love you. Drive safe."

"Love you too, Mom."

Tiffany went back into the room to gather her items. She snapped a few pictures of her beloved before kissing her softly on her cheek. "I love you, Granny. Always and forever," whispered Tiffany before making her way through the home. As Tiffany made her way through the house, she found herself taking in its sights and smells as she exited the door to her car and off to work.

She arrived around 9:30 am to a desk piled with work and coworkers who gave her the space she needed to just to be. One by one, she was greeted with a soft embrace and warm condolences as no one really knew what to say. Tiffany was the youngest in this small office of women. Right now, they were the moms and aunts she needed to survive the hours to come.

Two hours passed. Tiffany instinctively checked her phone every five minutes for updates and to respond to texts and well wishes. Her phone rang, and it was her mother.

"Hey, Mom." Tiffany's heart raced. She pushed her chair back to step away from her desk for another quick break.

"Hey. Tammy is there with Aunt Ann and Zora. The Elders are going to come to pray with her. They say it's going to be soon." She did it. Maribel got through the words on her very first call about her dying mother.

"Okay. I'm leaving work and heading down there. I'll call you when I get there."

"Okay, babe. I love you."

"I love you too."

This time it felt just a little stronger. The love, the intent, the meaning held each of them together just a moment longer.

When Tiffany arrived, she was greeted by Aunt Tammy, Zora, a family friend, Aunt Ann, another sister of Sharon's, and three elders from Sharon's congregation. The Elders were there to pray over her grandmother in her last moments. What a sight to see. Never in a million years did Tiffany *ever* imagine herself in this moment.

They all sat around her bedside, staring at the muted television. Tiffany scanned the room and noticed no one was watching the TV; just a room full of low gazes over the screen nearly hypnotized by the bitterness of this harsh reality.

Sharon's breathing became more and more labored. She struggled and gasped for each breath as if she was still holding on to the possibility of life — of true healing. A wave of silence swept the room as each space between her breaths became more substantial, more real.

Tiffany attempted to use the restroom a few times but was unsuccessful as other families were visiting and there were only two bathrooms to accommodate. She tried again anyway. She met Aunt Ann in the hallway, and they waited for the restroom together. They consoled each other and shared quick stories about their beloved grandmother and big sister. They sat on the ledge of the window in the dining area. They waited what seemed like fifteen minutes, where they shared in a few laughs and admired how beautiful the home was. Sharon would have been proud there.

Zora came out into the lobby and made eyes with Tiffany and Aunt Ann. Then, without saying a word, she nodded her head, blinked her eyes, and subtly summoned the two of them to the room. That was it. Sharon passed away at 1:39 pm on a Monday in May.

Tiffany could not bring herself to enter the room, but she had to get her phone. She had to call her mom. She walked in and placed her hand near her head, blocking her grandmother from her eyesight. She reached for her bag and glanced quickly at her beloved. Tiffany bid her sweet dreams and made her way out of the home and down the street.

She tried so hard to contain it, but Tiffany had the breakdown that had been looming over her shoulder for months. She walked down the road into a cull de sac trying to make sense of the moment they'd been anticipating for months. Nothing could quite prepare her for the depth of pain that she finally was forced to surrender to.

She was met shortly after by Cousin Marshall, who was visiting in from New York for Mirabel's birthday festivities. Marshall caught Tiffany on her way down and met her with a warm embrace. He held on to his baby cousin for as long as it was necessary to shield her from the pain ahead.

Sharon's death was a hard blow for everyone because Sharon hadn't been sick on that level. At least that's what everyone thought. Tiffany didn't know what to do with herself at this point. She had spent the last three months practically living on the third floor of the hospital. She knew the Intensive Care Unit staff, and their shift start and end times. Tiffany knew what time they came to reposition her grandmother, and even when her next medicine dose was due. She was right there for every minute of it. She lived on hospital coffee, hot Cheetos from the vending machine, and fast food delights from when friends would visit. She set up an area complete with her pillow, blanket, and laptop so she could do homework. She was attending her last set of classes at the local college before transferring. She was a busy young lady but made it her responsibility to be there for her grandmother every step of the way. Today she was relieved of her duties. The family decided to meet over Grandma Bella's home to discuss arrangements.

Her funeral would be a week later. Sharon's service would take place at her local Kingdom Hall, where family and friends would gather to pay their respects to the family. She would be cremated as this was her choice, and ashes would be split between her daughters. The repast took place at Mirabel's home, where most family and friends attended. The Witnesses from Sharon's congregation planned a separate repast. Tammy and Mirabel attended to express their gratitude for the outpour of love they received for their mother, a Witness of nearly thirty years.

Back at Mirabel's home, family and friends gathered to enjoy an evening of celebration in honor of Sharon. A close family friend of Tiffany's offered her voice as a gift to the family. She sang Sharon's favorite song by her favorite artist: Etta James' *At Last*.

At last, my love has come along,
My Lonely days are over, and life is like a song, oh yeah,
At last, the skies above are blue,
My heart was wrapped up in clover the night I looked at you,
I found a dream that I can speak to,
A dream that I can call my own,
I found a thrill to press my cheek to,
A thrill that I've never known,
You smiled and then the spell was cast,
And here we are in Heaven,
For you are mine at last.

Not a dry eye in sight. The lyrics of the melody were the perfect send-off for a soul ready to be reunited with the love of her life. Mirabel and Tammy's father had preceded her in death many years before. We all believed her heart never fully recovered from that. That day they met again, at last.

Chapter 9: Summer of Love

CARA

My big sister's funeral was beautiful. The family came together, and we all wore blue in her honor. It was lovely and a little unsettling that the next one might be without me. Nonetheless, I continued my fight. The outpouring of love our family received at that time had been so gratifying. Near and far, we connected ourselves through group chats and Facebook updates. No matter the outlet, we kept everyone in the loop. That day-to-day bonding changed something in us. It highlighted a genuine need in this family — a need to be loved and nurtured. Everyone came together to provide this for each other.

A few weeks before Sharon's passing, we got news that my mother, Bella, also had her own form of cancer she was battling. Her faith never wavered, and that was the spark that kept me going. Hers was a bit less aggressive, and she could take chemo shots to help. Other than day-to-day weakness, mentally, she was still sharp as a tack and loved to smile and laugh with her family. My mother and I bonded during this time. Mommy had this innate ability to make you feel warm inside just by looking upon her angelic face.

The months after my sister's passing was nothing short of an eerie peace that left us all hungover with disbelief. Life marched on the minute after she passed. Crazy how that works. You pray against these moments — that they never come, that they don't penetrate as deep as the last bit of pain did — but when it comes, it's there and then it's gone. You're forced to formulate new prayers, new peace, and a new life after the trauma.

Losing our eldest sibling was, in fact, traumatic. Still, it truly brought my siblings together in a fashion that I had missed for many years. Tragedy has a way of doing that, unfortunately.

My doctor was feeling positive about my outcome. I was feeling more energetic those days, more like myself, to be honest. Aside from walking a bit slower, my tenacity had returned, and I was determined to see this through. I pulled Carli out of traditional school. It was too much to deal with while staying at my mother's. Also, I couldn't rely on the twins to help me as they were transitioning into adulthood and trying to figure life out themselves. I was the source of our demise as a family, so my approach to just let them be was best, trust me.

I looked forward to possibly moving back to my place full time at the end of the summer. I thought it was time. At that point, being at my mom's was good for me because it kept me in high spirits. Carli was here with me, and we were close to my doctor and hospital of choice.

The girls were living a life of freedom with no consequences as they were eighteen and thought the world revolved around them. I just didn't have the energy to fight them on any of this.

The last time we battled as a family, Brianna threatened to take Carli and run if I did not commit to rehab. She was so upset she posted our entire household business online for the world to see. She was sixteen, and I was on a path of destruction. The family was not impressed with any of this.

Today things were becoming better between us; however, I was feeling guilty for the events of their lives. I struggled with being a friend, let alone a parent. Nonetheless, our family had been my pillar of strength.

We all became so close that last year, it was a dream come true. Grandma had seen some of her distant grandchildren and had spent memorable moments being the matriarch of us all. This time had been beautiful in that we really stepped up for each other. I kept a close watch on my baby, Carli. She made some friends in my mother's complex and spent her days up under me and outdoors in the evening. I was trying to give her some sort of normalcy in her adolescent life. Our new normal was this place of uncertainty. We were making the best of it all, and for that, I was proud.

The summer was here, and my mom's sisters came to town from New York for a visit.

Generations of love were here in one place. My mother's smile was one I would never forget. Her smile reminded me of my own, a level of love and peace within myself, a love of self that I finally felt in my passing days. I had this urge to get together with family, to eat good food, and gather in a place of comfort and celebrate life. So that's what we did. I put the call out to Mirabel.

"Hello."

"Hey, Bel Bel." That was my nickname for her, which she grew to love. "I was thinking, since Aunt Angie and Aunt Rita are in town, we should do a barbeque or something at the house. What do you think?"

Mirabel, smiled through the phone, "I would love that. We need some family time now that things have calmed down! Let's shoot for Sunday!"

"Okay, great! Yes, we do, and your house is the perfect place for everyone! I'll put the word out and have everyone bring something."

"Don't worry about it too much. We'll throw something on the grill and I'll do a few sides and —"

"You're making your famous mac and cheese, right?"

We laughed. "Yes, you know I will!"

We hung up and spread the word of the impromptu family gathering at Mirabel's on Sunday at three.

The family gathered that Sunday. Mirabel, in fact, did make her famous mac and cheese. My goodness, it was by far the best mac and cheese I'd ever had. Flavors meant something more to me those days; They meant existence. Taste, the five senses, the feeling of living all in one bite. I was enjoying this time with my family. I was enjoying life. The laughter went on and on; The love went even further.

Tiffany disappeared with the girls for a bit and returned with a tattoo in memory of her grandmother. I was very shocked at her choice to get tattoos as a Capricorn, but I'll leave my astrology woes for later. It was a simple and classic "Forever Love" with a heart on her wrist. The twist was that it was in my sister Sharon's writing. How rad! What a beautiful way to honor her grandmother.

Mirabel and Tammy seemed to be handling Sharon's passing well. Mirabel and I often spoke about Sharon and about life in general. I enjoyed her perspective. I mean, she was the oldest niece and oldest granddaughter, she had seen it all.

The night was young, and I took my place in the kitchen — cleaning and organizing the leftovers — a role I'd become accustomed to. Mirabel did so much when it came to the cooking, hosting, and opening her home, the least I could do was clean up. As usual, she told me not to worry about it; She'd take care of it later. In true form, I laughed, ignored her, and continued with my extensive cleaning routine. We were family; your mess was my mess.

Chapter 10: Amen

CARA

Maybe that family gathering was exactly what I needed. Perhaps that very day was what my soul needed to finally say goodbye. As harsh as my reality was, my journey was one I would remain proud of. Two weeks ago, the smiles of my family and the happiness in my girls became my reason to continue this fight.

I stared into blinking monitors and flashing lights. I was back in the hospital.

The last two nights, I ran a fever, got progressively weaker and far more agitated. I checked in at midnight last night. The minute they removed my wig, I *felt* like a cancer patient. My body went weak, the essence of my being depleted with each stick, each prod, and each poke.

The optimism I once had disappeared as the hum of my doctor's undertone remained bleak. He stared blankly at my latest blood panel. I guessed that the cancer had spread. It had to have spread because, at this point, I no longer felt like myself. It hurt to smile, and nothing was remotely funny. I was angry. I was losing.

The next few days were a blur. I had visitors; Old friends coming in to keep me company. They all wondered where my kids were. I must have looked a lot worse than what they let on.

"Hey, Mirabel. It's Ella. I'm here at the hospital and Cara isn't looking too good. The girls should really be here visiting. Have you talked to them?"

"Hey, Ella. I'll reach out again. I've let them know she's back in, but Cara doesn't want anyone saying anything to her girls right now. So, it's a difficult situation."

"I understand, and she told me the same thing and was really adamant about it too. That's why I decided to call you. It seems like it could be soon."

"Oh, wow. Okay. I was planning on coming down tonight. I'll call Brianna and let her know they should get down there and spend some time with her."

That night Mirabel and Farrell came to see me. I was up to having them visit as the morning was uneventful and filled with pain management injections and tests. Being around them was always uplifting. We spoke about Mirabel's daycare, how everyone in the family is doing, and my girls. I'm not sure why everyone was so concerned about them, they would come when they could. It was difficult for everyone to understand and accept the dynamics I had with *my* children. However, they must respect it, especially at this time, let me have control of this one thing.

Over the next few days, Mirabel had a conversation with Brianna to let her know the severity of the end of my fight.

"Hey, Brianna. It's Mirabel. I wanted to talk to you to see how you're doing and if you've gone to see your mom. And where is Carli?"

"Hey, cousin. Carli is with Roger and his family." It made Mirabel a little uneasy that Carli had spent the week with Cara's boyfriend's family, but she was safe and cared for, and that is all that mattered.

"Brianna —"

"Mirabel, please excuse my language but cut the bullshit. Give it to me straight what's going on."

"Okay. Your mom isn't doing well. You guys should get Carli and go see her and spend time with her."

"But the doctors said she was doing well. I thought this hospital visit was just for her fever?"

"It's more involved than that, baby. She's very sick. And even though she may tell you she's okay, she's not and would love to see you guys."

Brianna and Carli visited me that night. I did not want them to see me like this, but there we were. Carli cradled into my chest and snuggled until she fell asleep. Brianna and I sat and talked while watching E! News together. It was peaceful.

Alana had cramps and wanted to rest at home.

I took that moment to reflect as I felt a feeling of peace over me. I was breathing. I felt my child's warmth against my skin. I was looking at my eldest child with all of her beauty, brains, and stamina. That would take her far in this life. I saw myself and hoped and prayed to God that they followed a better truth than the one I provided for them growing up.

I told them I was getting tired and wanted to rest, that I would see them this weekend. I lied. I just couldn't handle this in-between space of being their mother and a soon-to-be distant memory. What do you fill the silence with when words don't come so easy?

I spent that Thursday playing phone tag with Alana and Brianna. I called Mirabel several times that day — mostly just to say "hi." I called Farrell the same amount. I just needed comfort.

It was getting harder to breathe. My hands quivered with pain as I attempted to pick up the remote. And my skin? My skin was leathered with exhaustion; Wilted from the drugs (not the chemo drugs). The lines that intersect my arms were bursting through my thinned skin. Go figure, I spent my entire life developing thick skin, but today, I laid there defeated. My bones hurt. They ached with pain that was so deep, so confined, and so unreachable that *doing nothing* was doing too much. My hand was permanently glued to my pain button. I took a hit every few minutes. Even though the dosing was low, having that instant control over my body brought me joy. I felt honored to have that last bit of control even in that state. My cheeks were sunken, and my lips dry and cracked. I hadn't bathed in days, a sponge bath is just not the same. So, I just laid there and waited.

Dr. Olson called Mirabel that evening. He informed her that the time would be near. That he anticipated my passing within the next few days; my organs were beginning to fail, and I was growing weaker.

They were attending the wedding of some close friends not too far from the hospital. With new love in the air, Mirabel, Farrell, and Tiffany came to the hospital in hopes of uplifting me. They gave me a hug that I think we all needed. When they walked in, what they saw was not what they expected. The nurses cleared the room and revealed a very sick me. I was virtually unrecognizable, weakened in mind, body, and now finally weakened in my fighting spirit.

"They said —" I struggled to string together a sentence, but the words sifted through my chattering teeth. "They — they said I am not going to make it."

Mirabel looked to Tiffany and Farrell.

"Tiffany, go ahead and step out for a second while I talk with Cara."

Tiffany grabbed my hand and held it tight. "Smile for me, Aunty. Please."

My smile was magnetic and electrifying, to say the least. I mustered up the biggest most beautiful smile I could. Then Tiffany released her hand and walked out of the room.

Farrell and Mirabel spoke quietly at my bedside.

"What about my girls?" I faintly questioned the fate of my offspring.

Mirabel sat at my bedside, holding my hand, feeling my warmth in her palm. She felt the life of her beloved aunt slipping away as the moment passed. Mirabel whispered into my ear, "It's okay, Cara. I will make sure the girls will be okay. I promise."

Mirabel and I and both closed our eyes and let the tears fall. Farrell consoled us both. Tiffany made her way back into the room, where she too joined in on the hug of all hugs.

They left that evening, knowing the time would come soon. Mirabel let the family know that the inevitable was upon us.

My mother had made peace with all of this days ago. She said she did not want to see me in this state, that she'd rather see me healthy in the new system. Same for my brother. Hell, I was glad they kept me away from mirrors.

When Mirabel, Farrell, and Tiffany left, the nurses filed in to distribute my medicine and to give me a sponge bath. It's incredible how much they seem to care even though I was dying. The water felt so amazing on my skin, cleansing mostly. After my bath, my frail body was carefully placed back in the hospital's nightgown. I was back to laying and thinking about my life, how I got here, and what I hoped to leave behind.

A few hours later, around 11:30 PM, my girls came. Brianna with her boyfriend and Alana with hers. The four of them entered the room as I was vomiting. The moment was here, and they witnessed every bit of it just like they have everything else in their lives. I mouthed in between gags, "I'm sorry." Brianna rushed over to console me while Alana rushed to get the nurse.

Brianna held my hand. She just kept telling me how much she loved me. In and out of consciousness, I met her gaze, and at that moment, I knew she did. After all I put them through — the failed rehab attempts, the fights, their dad, all of my downfalls as a parent — it meant nothing at that moment. I was their mother. They were my children. And we did our best.

I died late that night. Nothing about this journey could've prepared me for these last moments with my children. The weighted sadness that I could do nothing about but surrender to was growing. Death wasn't as painful as I thought; It was a clearing of energy, of thought, and of want. It was magnified peace, and everything became clear, beautiful, and tranquil. My time expired on this earth on a warm summer night in August. I prayed my decisions up to that point were not made in vain and that my children could be surrounded by the love they deserve from the family who stepped up at that time.

Well, I made it to heaven. I think. Not sure if I should be here, but I guess cancer gives you the golden ticket. My funeral service was beautiful. My family showed out. My friends filled the seats of the very same church where we had my husband's service. Never in a million years did I imagine me watching my own funeral, a bird's eye view of my life told through the stories of the people I'd touched. Imagine that. I actually impacted the lives of so many people with just my smile.

Jerry, my old neighbor, spoke about the time we did a late-night beach run, half of which I have no recollection of, but what a memory! Tiffany, my niece, spoke about our Capricorn bond. The reflection of my face on my children. How the family honored me by taking care of my girls. Wow. Not a dry eye in sight. My picture was one from a good chemo day, my smile looked painless.

My mother was dressed in her matching hat and heels, and my family dressed so elegantly and beautifully while sitting up front. They all sat wondering how we got here but embraced it as best we could. Now I waited, watched, and prayed that Mirabel and the girls honored our legacy of love. Love in the time of crisis was our thing; at least that's what I thought.

MIRABEL

I walked down the stairs of my home. The darkness in the stairway seemed minuscule to the darkness in my spirit. Despite the feeling, I found my way to Tiffany's room and delivered another gut-wrenching update.

"Cara passed."

Our eyes briefly met as she nodded and maneuvered slowly off her bed. Her eyes darted to the clock on her nightstand: 12:05 AM.

Delivering this news became the new normal for my daughter and me. Many times during this process, she had been my rock. Her strength often shocked me as I saw her juggle becoming a young woman overcoming her own tribulations yet remaining strong and compassionate for others. At that moment, I needed to know she was okay. That we were okay, our brief silent exchange reassured me that yet again, we would get through this.

I made my way back upstairs. The moment we had all been sluggishly anticipating came and went just like that. In my bathroom, I sat numb and nearly lifeless. The stillness of the night was oddly comforting as this was to be one of the only moments of clarity over the next days, weeks, and months.

My favorite aunt was gone. I just couldn't believe how hard this had been, and to lose my own mother along the way, one's heart could only take so much.

Two significant deaths in six months. *I know I'm strong, Jehovah, but I don't know how much I can handle.* My aunt's passing was expected; however, are you ever really fully prepared to say goodbye to *anyone* prematurely? My life was about to change drastically. More importantly, I was responsible for the care and livelihood of another human being, my cousin. A new mother of a thirteen-year-old child. Our roles would change from cousins to parent/child. And from this point, I would raise her exactly as my own. The promise I made to my aunt was one of the most important commitments I intended to honor with grace.

I missed my mom. I wished I had her here to consult with because I knew this was going to be challenging. Despite her reservations about the matter, I went ahead and moved forward with guardianship plans. I was determined not to let our baby cousin get lost in the system. I still remember the conversation. My mom was in the hospital, and we spoke on the phone about it, and even though we were miles apart, I could see the starkness on her face as she cut me off mid-sentence.

"Don't do it, Mirabel." In that subtle, graceful way she does to put her foot down and proverbially end the conversation.

"Mom, there's no one else. We have the space and are able to financially. Besides, Cara asked me personally, Mom."

"Mmm." Every black mother's staple response when she's heard enough.

"I've prayed about it. Farrell and I have talked about it. We've been talking about it with Tiffany and Drew. And Drew is so excited to have someone close to his age in the house!"

"I just wish one of my brothers or sisters would step up. Cara and her kids, man. I just don't trust it. Besides, you'll have to deal with the twins in a way that may frustrate you, and you may just have a lot to deal with in general. That's all I'm saying. As your mom, this is my last piece of advice."

She giggled, and we moved on to another subject.

That conversation stuck with me, not because she was concerned but because I could only hope to have the support and backing of my aunts and uncles as the roles changed for us. We were fully prepared to do this alone. Hell, I've been a mother since I was fifteen. I got this.

PART TWO

The caged bird sings with a fearful trill, of things unknown, but longed for still, and his tune is heard on the distant hill, for the caged bird sings of freedom.

Maya Angelou

Chapter 11: Year One

MIRABEL

When I said, "I got this," I meant it. Soon after Cara passed, to avoid slipping into any further sadness and defeat, I channeled my energy into doing what I did best: handle business. I got right on the phone, gathered documents, sent out letters, waited for hours on hold, all to begin the process of guardianship for my baby cousin. Since Cara's passing, Carli had been with her sisters as they were getting her ready to move to our place in the few weeks before school started.

My husband and I prayed about this daily since accepting responsibility. His only request: "WE'RE NOT MOVING!"

My husband knew me so well. With Tiffany in the downstairs granny flat and secondary daycare space, and Drew upstairs in the main house with us, I was determining whether we should move or not. Farrell made it clear that we would, in fact, make it work with the space we had. For now, we planned for Carli and Drew to share a room. We would reassess in a few months. The foundation was set for what I was hoping to be a smooth transition.

Back to the legal guardianship.

In the state of California, there were several steps to obtain legal guardianship of a minor. The blessing and the curse were that both parents were deceased. We didn't necessarily have to petition the surviving parent; however, the process was still very much that, a process.

A legal guardian acts as the primary caretaker of the child or minor, in this case, Carli. The guardian may be selected by biological parents or appointed by the court. Given that Justin was deceased, Cara selected Farrell and me as primary caretakers of Carli. However, we were to give access to her sisters, which we'll discuss later. We obtained the same responsibilities to care for Carli just as we would our own by providing full legal and physical custody of her. We were also responsible for making the decision about the physical care of Carli. These responsibilities included food, clothing, shelter, safety, protection, physical and emotional growth, medical and dental care, education, and special needs care. Sounded about right.

Oh, here was my favorite, we were responsible for her supervision and could be held liable for any intentional damages she may cause. Oh jeez. Well, I intended to treat her like my own and hoped that she understood that our roles shifted from cousins to parent, and that's just the way it had to be, at least for the next five years.

I'd like to think I was a good mother. I did the best I could, and my girl turned out pretty damn good. Raising my son with my husband had been the biggest treat yet. I imagined that's why Cara chose me. She always complimented me on Tiffany, on how sweet she was, and how grateful she was her girls had someone positive to look up to. I was proud of that.

Over the next week or so, Farrell and I became literal paper pushers as we gathered documents needed to present to the courts to prove our capability to take in another child. There were so many documents, please forgive me if I forgot a few: petition for appointment of guardian, guardianship petition, notice of hearing, consent of proposed guardian, duties of guardian, letters of guardianship, declaration under uniform child custody jurisdiction and enforcement act, confidential guardian screening form, and order appointing guardian. Pretty much a giant packet of tiny print that we both read and signed.

Next, we had the forms reviewed for errors and filed with the County Clerk. A notice was given to the Social Security Administration. We then submitted to a home investigation as well as background checks for all adults in the home, Tiffany included. These were already in place due to the home daycare I run, but we submitted them anyways to prevent any missteps.

Before the summer was over, we attended two weekends of parenting classes on the joys of raising children into teens, understanding their emotions, and relating to them in productive and positive ways. Our home was inspected, again — a reoccurring phenomenon as my daycare license requires frequent home inspections. Still, we obliged and pass the inspection with flying colors.

Now that we had Drew's room arranged to add her twin-sized bed, Carli was set to move in that weekend. She had her twin bed and nightstand she brought from her sisters. I went to Ross and got her a few decorative pillows, a pink throw, and a journal. (I've always encouraged the young ladies in the family to write their thoughts out good or bad as a safe space.) I thought to make it nice and welcoming with little girly touches that I knew she'd like.

She was starting school up here in a week. She was about a month late, but her counselors understood the circumstance. We had *a lot* of work to do to get these grades up to the ninth-grade level. I knew Cara let her homeschool the last six months, but I doubted anyone really kept up with her and her schoolwork because those grades were terrible. F's and D's, yet she passed the eighth grade.

Anyways, due to the circumstance of which she transferred to her new high school, counselors met with Farrell and me and suggested she attend counseling offered by their department. Given the loss of her father at a young age and just recently, her mother. We discussed it with Carli; she did not seem the least bit interested; in fact, she said she was excited to have a fresh start. So we decided we'd wait it out and see how it went. We gave her a chance to breathe and adjust to the house. We were cautious not to bombard with her too much as we were all still nurturing the crippling hole in our hearts from all the loss we just experienced.

The date was set, and we had everything arranged for Carli to move in with us in a week. We wanted to make sure everyone was on the same page, so we called a meeting with the girls, Carli, Farrell, and myself. We wanted to address any concerns, let them know we were there for them through this process, and let them know the agreement we came up with. It was decided by all of us that Carli would spend the weekends with her sisters. Farrell and I would be responsible for getting her to and from school and handle all the day-to-day responsibility of parenting. We decided to do it this way to afford the twins a chance at normal early adult life. As much as was possible up until this point. We knew they did not want to be parents to their thirteen-year-old sister. When the opportunity presented itself, they jumped at the idea of having us take Carli over them. None of this measured up to the reality that these young eighteen-year-old women were just not equipped to care for their baby sister.

"Carli, you understand that even though we are cousins, now the dynamics sort of shift. We have to be parents now. We want you to know we love you and are going to guide you like we would our own." I stated as I began the table talk.

"Yes, Carli. This is the best place for you. And we will be here anytime you need us. And we'll come to visit during the week and take you to lunch or something." Brianna said to reassure her sister. Carli's life had a chance at normalcy. Brianna kissed her forehead to say, "Embrace it, sis. You're home."

We wanted to make it just that, a home for her. We didn't have an extra bedroom, but we made it cute for her, and she loved it. When Brianna and Alana saw her new space, they jokingly begged to move in as well. We all laughed. Laughter was our thing.

A few weeks had gone by, and Carli seemed to adjust well. It had been two weeks since she'd seen her sisters. We wanted to give them some time on their own to grieve and to provide Carli with the time to adjust to the household, so we said we would resume weekend visits later. The time was also to give her sisters a chance to domesticate the home and develop their own routine post-Cara.

When she finally went down to her sisters for a three-day weekend, she came home singing a different tune. She was very distant, recluse. She had somewhat of an attitude. I'd seen this before with my own teen daughter, and I know exactly how to handle this. Later that night, when Farrell and Drew were at the grocery store, I decided to ask her how her weekend was.

"Carli! Come here when you get a sec!"

"Coming, Mirabel."

"How was your weekend? Did you have fun?"

"Yea, it was cool."

"Did you miss being with them?"

Tears were welling up behind her eyes as she answered faintly. "Yes." She started crying massive tears with no sound emerging from her mouth.

I got up from the bed and gave her a mother's hug. I asked if she thought she would rather be there with them during this time. Silence. I pulled her back from my chest. She nodded.

The next day I spoke with Farrell about our options. "The girl wants to be with her sisters right now, that's her comfort. How can we compete with that? With them, she has her friends, many of which she's known a few years. She has them and her home full of memories of her mother."

"And freedom, let's not forget freedom of not being watched by her preoccupied sisters."

"I get it. I just want what is best for her."

We called the twins up to our home later that week for yet another family meeting. We wanted to let them know where Carli was in regards to her happiness. We wanted to express to them that we would be willing to have her live with them, have them get her to and from school, and we would monitor as her guardians. As crazy as that seemed, I felt like as a family, together, we would figure it out. I knew Carli would change her mind. I had to give her time to adjust. I also needed her to understand that we had her back and were listening to her.

"I don't think a child should make that decision," Alana said matter of fact.

"We're not letting her make the decision, and let's not talk about Carli as if she isn't here. We just want to do what is best for her. She wants to be with who she's closest to, and that's her friends and you guys right now."

Brianna chimed in, "Carli, we love you, but living here is going to be what's best. We don't even have food in our fridge right now. Mirabel had to help us with rent this month." She said sort of laughing yet very serious.

"Yeah, Carli. Mom picked the best person for you. The best home to live in. And you're not losing us. We will be here weekly to see you and will be involved in all of your school activities. We promise."

"Carli?" Farrell asked, looking to her and looking back at the group.

"I want to stay! My sisters are right. This is the best place. And I do actually like my school and my teachers. I guess I can try it a little longer."

"See, we just wanted you to see both sides of it, you know we will be here for you if you need to talk, vent, cry—whatever we are here as your support. Okay?" I was optimistic.

"One more thing," Brianna said as we were wrapping up. "We were thinking that maybe we can get Carli every other weekend. Due to my work schedule, it would be easier to get her when we're off so we can spend time with her."

Farrell looked to me. I looked at Carli. "That's fine with me if it's okay with you, Carli."

"That's fine."

It was settled. Carli would stay with us in our home, share a room with Drew temporarily, attend school in this district, and see her sisters every other weekend at their place.

We also expressed to them that since we were her legal guardians, the same rules needed to apply for her at their place as it would for one of my own. "This means following curfew times, chores if they ask, and respect of the rules. All in agreement, say 'I.'"

"I." In unison, they sang.

A month or so had gone by, and we survived. We survived the major blackout of Southern California, the fires that seem to blaze every year, and two whole months with a teenager and pre-teen in the home.

Upon her arrival and agreement to stay with us full time, we had another discussion with Tiffany included. This time about the roles of each of us in the home. Carli would have chores just as Tiffany did and would have to stay on top of her school work once she got those grades up to high school level. My goal was to assimilate her into the home as seamless as I would a new baby. It felt good so far. As good as could be expected. I had no idea what to expect; all I knew was I would honor what I said. I would give her the life she deserved, the love she deserved, and the freedom to grow into a beautiful young lady just like her sisters. Everyone deserved a fair chance at happiness, I hoped we could bridge the gap for her.

The start of Carli's school year had been quite rocky. First, we had to assess her grades. My goal was to help her to understand that even though she was grieving, now was the time to buckle down, in memory of her mother. Counselors at the school had been great with helping me to navigate through all of this to ensure she got the help she needed. They walked her through the process, allowed her to pick her classes, and walked her through the campus to become familiar. They gave her pamphlets of different clubs, groups, and teams she might be interested in. They highlighted the need for extracurricular activities to keep her busy and mentioned it might be an excellent way to connect with other students. At least that's what we thought.

Carli found herself mixed in with a crowd that was, let's just say undesirable for any concerned parent. Shortly after her start at her new school, I received a call on my home landline from the office.

"Hello, Mrs. Davis? I am calling in regards to Ms. Carli. I have her here in the office."

"Alright," unsure of exactly what was coming next but encouraging her to proceed.

"Carli was in the bathroom with three other students, two of whom were caught with marijuana."

"WHAT?!" The words came slicing through my teeth.

"Ma'am, no one was caught smoking. However, we do have to have a parent come down to pick her up as we will have to proceed with disciplinary action for all parties involved. I hope you understand."

"Yes, absolutely! I understand. We will talk to her. I know the school is aware of her case, and I appreciate you handling this with care. But, this is *not* acceptable, especially in my home. I will be sure to have a chat with Ms. Carli when she gets home. "

"Thank you, Mrs. Davis. At this time, Carli must attend a drug and alcohol class for teens that we require students to attend when faced with situations like this."

"Understandable, we will be there shortly to pick her up."

Hanging up, I called upstairs to Farrell. He rushed down into the daycare, and I began to explain the fun we had ahead. He went to the school to pick her up, and we started on the journey as parents to a very lost young lady.

When she arrived home, she sauntered in slow and drawn inward. Dark energy exuding from her pores. Oh, she thought this would be enough just to be sent to her room? Think again, Miss Thang. Farrell registered her for her drug classes to begin this Saturday and Sunday. Two weekends. Eight hours a day of drug and alcohol talk.

When asked who the friends were. She stood there. When asked why she thought it was okay to be in the bathroom doing all that. She stared blankly. When asked if this was the route she wanted to go down starting at a new school. She slowly shook her head 'no.' When asked if she had anything to say for herself, she faintly whispered, "Sorry."

Later that night, Farrell and I had our powwow of how to proceed with her. We wondered when to tell her sisters. The goal was to prevent the trickle of this behavior on to Drew, our son. The two had developed quite the bond over the last few weeks. Carli had to be mindful of the example she was now setting being an older sibling in the home versus the baby with her sisters.

Carli successfully completed her classes and vowed to choose better friends at school. We encouraged her to try out for the school's cheer team since her sisters cheered. When I mentioned it, her face lit up. I knew it would be something she'd enjoy. Besides, the comradery and sisterhood of a cheer team would be so beneficial for her right now. I took her down to the tryouts and watched her completely transform when the spotlight was on her. It was amazing! I knew that she needed to do this, she needed to have this space to release and be free. We would do anything we could to help.

We found out a week later that she made the team! She actually made junior varsity as a freshman and could possibly be varsity by next year. Wow! She was so excited to share with her sisters! We had a lovely family dinner that night. She loved sitting and watching us cook in the kitchen.

That night I pulled her aside and let her know how incredibly proud of her I was and that she had real talent as a cheerleader. She smiled and said she was so excited to learn the dance portion and how she couldn't wait to perform. She said she wished she could share this with her mom. My heart sank into my stomach. I let her know that she could always talk to me about her mom and that she could use the journal I got her to write letters to her mom to stay close with her. She loved the idea and retreated back to hanging with Drew. I prayed that night for our journey ahead for me to do my very best at this. I know my aunt heard my prayers.

Dear Jehovah,

Thank you for your grace in our lives. I pray that Carli continues down the right path. I pray that we can guide her in the right way the way her mother would. I pray she appreciates what we have been asked to do. And I pray that you cover us in your will along the way. Please protect my family near and far.

In Jesus' name, we pray. Amen.

Mirabel

Dear Mommy,

I miss you! I made the cheer team at my new high school. I know you would be proud because I'm following in the steps of my sisters. I like it here at Mirabel's. Tonight Farrell made stir fry, and it was so amazing. Drew is fun to hang with. Mirabel makes the best pancakes LOL. I miss you, Mom, but I'm doing okay. I'm meeting new friends and super excited for the family to come to see me cheer for our first game. I love you, Mom.

Carli-bear.

Chapter 12: Year Two

MIRABEL

Our first year as a new family unit was challenging, to say the least. Co-parenting with Carli's twin sisters, my baby cousins, had not been ideal, but we made the necessary adjustments. Neither of us predicted this to be our future, so we rolled with issues as they came.

Carli seemed to be doing well in school now that she understood that I was not the one to play with. She quickly came to understand two things: one, I was not above the law. A mantra that I poured into my own children, letting *them* know I could only do so much as Mom. Once they broke the law, I couldn't help them. Two, I saw right through her teen lies and ways of manipulation. So, honesty was always the best policy, at least when dealing with me.

Our day-to-day routine ran as follows: I opened my in-home daycare by 6:30 AM. I got the kids up to make sure they got ready. I woke my husband up and went downstairs to begin my day. Farrell then resumed the responsibility of dropping the kids off. One stop to the middle school for Drew and another stop to the high school for Carli.

Carli always loved to ride shotgun. With her being the oldest, we often let her. She always loved to talk to whoever was driving about random stuff. That was her moment to be free, and we encouraged it.

Farrell would then, on most days, pick me up a cup of coffee and donut when he wanted to make me smile. We would chat together in my tiny daycare and have our morning coffee together. I looked forward to these moments because it connected us for the day. Our dynamics changed as husband and wife since taking Carli in. Those stolen quiet moments were so much more special those days.

We afforded ourselves the luxury of being able to work from home. Him in financial services and me a business owner. We loved the freedom but worked very hard and long hours to provide for our family. When he went off to his office, I tended to the children I cared for.

Once the school day let out, he then rounded the troops. First Drew, then a bank run for me, errands, swoop around after cheer practice to pick up Carli and home to start dinner.

He cooked more for the family during the week since I got off later; this worked for our family. The kids loved the creations he came up with. Carli enjoyed family dinners. This wasn't something she was used to with my aunt, let alone full course meals. Once their father passed, the family dynamic was hard to fully grasp. Things of this nature became few and far between.

We let the kids pick a favorite meal for special occasions. Carli always picked my chicken and waffles. She loved Farrell's breakfast spread he'd make for us on Sundays. Carli even asked to cook for the family every now and then. She really blossomed into a beautiful young lady. With her now being the oldest in the home versus the baby, she loved the independence from her sisters and the freedom from her past.

Her sophomore year started off smoothly. We all got together to see her cheer for her first homecoming game. Her sisters, their boyfriends, and a few proud friends came to cheer her on. Also in tow were Tiffany, Drew, myself, Farrell, and my sister Tammy and her dog Bentley. We all showed up to support Carli. She did a fantastic job. We were so proud to see her out there, honoring exactly what her mom would've wanted for her. Seeing her out there, her sisters cheered and cried tears of joy. They cried when they saw how happy and well-received their baby sister was, man was she popular!

I'm not sure how many new faces we met that evening, but it felt so good to see her shine and know that she was happy. She was most excited to introduce the family to her best friend. A young lady named Allison. Cute girl, a blonde with green eyes, and also a cheerleader. Allison was new to California, and she and Carli hit it off right away. I had heard great things about Allison and was glad we got to meet her. I was even happier Carli had a close friend.

Carli's freshman year was a rough start as far as her grades went. With the right pep talk, we were able to help her to understand that she had to keep her grades up to stay in cheer and any other extracurricular activities. That seemed to do the trick. She did not want to give up cheer, so she hit the books.

At this time, Drew was in middle school and getting ready to join Carli in high school. Oddly enough, they knew many of the same kids and bonded in ways that Drew needed at the time. Carli loved playing big sis. They giggled nightly over social media videos, shared inside jokes, and understood each other in ways only two Geminis could. Carli confided in Drew about boys, Drew poked fun at her like a little brother should. They bickered at times, but for the most part, you could find them both lying on the floor in my living room on their phones, looking at funny videos with a bag of chips between the two of them, TV blaring. I knew how special those moments were for Drew. He and Tiffany were thirteen years apart. He and Iman, Farrell's daughter, my bonus daughter, were eight years apart. He never had that in-home sibling relationship. Carli's presence was special for all of us.

Alana and Brianna did the best they could considering. They got Carli every other weekend or whenever they could. Some weekends they did. Some they didn't. Either way, we understood and tried to make Carli understand as well. They were going on twenty years old and just lost their mother. Now they were forced to live this life the best way they could. They had a lot of help from Alana's boyfriend's family, who stepped in and did what our family was unable to.

After helping them with their rent a few times, Farrell and I had to shift our focus to making sure Carli had what she needed here. Their family bought Brianna a car and would have gotten one for Alana had she wanted to drive. Right now, Alana was in this space of just wanting to be up under Brianna, who is the more independent of the two.

I was just glad they were both working in between all the partying they did. Hell, without parents, their house was the 'kick it' spot for their friends. Nonetheless, the bills got paid, and I could only trust that they were following the rules we set for Carli when she was with them on the weekends she did go.

We had a few issues with them when Carli was down there visiting. Issues resulting in arguments on when to bring her home, what they allow her to do, and overall competition for parental control. It was challenging. A lot more challenging than I expected. For the most part, they respect me and what I asked. It was just those few times they tried to push the envelope and just did what they want with *their* sister. I went from a respected cousin to the bad guy when it came to the rules I set for Carli in this house. But whatever, I had a job to do and not letting her fall into the system was the first one.

Tiffany and Brianna had gotten so close during this time. At one point, Tiffany was going to move in with them to help them with the bills and give us more space here for Carli. Tiffany quickly decided that wasn't the move for her, given all the extra activity they had going on there. I didn't blame her, besides I would hate for anything like that to destroy what they had as cousins. I knew nothing like that would ever happen to this family. We'd been through so much. All we had was each other.

We developed a new Christmas tradition the year Aunt Cara was diagnosed. Tiffany and I decided at that time that we all needed a fun night of light energy and good food, so we had everyone over on Christmas Eve. I made my famous chicken and waffles, and Tiffany made holiday cocktails. We played the Wii and took pictures by the tree to send Aunt Cara while she was in the hospital. We vowed then to make this a yearly tradition for the cousins. And we did just that. We kept true to the tradition the first year with Carli and now again during our second.

This year, the cousins each made a dish for sharing. I was making the dessert. Tiffany prepared appetizers and cocktails.

The Gingerbread house contest that Tiffany started last year commenced. The cousins broke off into teams to decorate their houses. Farrell, Tiffany, and I judged the contest. We played holiday music, our favorite neo-soul hits, and we spent the evening eating, drinking, and being merry. And pictures? We didn't forget the pictures. That's one thing we did, and we did *well*. We showcased all the fun on our social media pages to include distant family in the fun. My home was the spot for gatherings and love, and I was thrilled that even after all the sadness, we had a stable place to let loose and be free. This Christmas was a special one in particular. For the last four months, Farrell had been busy in the garage building a room for Ms. Carli. With two teens in the home, they both needed their space. So, to prevent us from moving, he came up with this. My husband, I tell ya! He did it, though. He built Carli a room complete with a closet, lighting, windows, carpeting, and insulation. We planned to have it done for Christmas and asked her sisters and family to cater her Christmas gifts to decorate her new space. She was now on the same floor as Tiffany's room and my daycare. Since Farrell hardly used the garage, his home office would move upstairs to our room, and she would have access to the rest of the house as usual. We planned to decorate it and present it to her as her final big gift on Christmas day.

"Okay Carli, we have one more gift for you, it's downstairs in the garage, we can all go down and see, but you have to close your eyes..."

All of us, including her sisters, walked her down the stairs and into the garage. We stood around her, opened her room door slowly, and quietly uncovered her blindfold.

All in unison, "One. Two. Three!"

Carli's eyes widened with excitement and tears streamed down her face, "Is this for me?!"

Farrell and I shook our heads together.

"I thought you were building a man cave, oh my goodness! Thank you!" she hugged all of us and jumped into her bed.

"Wow, Car, you're so lucky! I'm like, can I move in here?!" Brianna laughed as she gave her baby sis a kiss.

We all laughed and relished in Carli's excitement. I was glad we could all be here for this moment. Sticking together was our thing.

Chapter 13: Years Three and Four

MIRABEL

You know how they say you never know someone's true colors until you live with them? Well, they were absolutely right. I was living in a home with two teenagers, and both of them were driving me insane. Between trying to get my son on track with his grades and keeping up with Carli's hygiene concerns, lies, and teen drama, I was at my wits end trying to find peace.

Let's see, over the last eight months, Carli had some significant issues come up. One was a huge fight with her best friend Allison, the one we met at the football game. Let's just say there was drama over a boy. Drama that Carli had no business being part of. Drama that she caused and ultimately had to face.

Carli came to me one day crying, distraught, and eager to tell her side. Alison had a boyfriend that Carli thought was cute. Here we go. Carli decided to pursue this boy behind Alison's back. Eventually, Alison and the boy broke up, and he and Carli began talking. The friendship with Alison went to shit, and the boy went back to Alison shortly after Carli. I thought *Melrose Place* was juicy.

Anyways, in talking with Carli, I knew how upset she was about it. Still, I had to explain to her what boundaries were within friendships, especially when boys were involved. She explained to me that she really cared about this guy even after only knowing him for a few days. I asked her to write out her thoughts, to process her feelings and maybe write Alison a letter. She didn't want to lose Alison, but she knew this would put a strain on things.

Things calmed down in Carli's world just long enough to make it to spring break. She was becoming a bit more popular in the cheer world. The Alison crisis worked itself out, and they made up eventually. However, more catty behavior presented itself, which became the demise of her cheer career.

Carli got into trouble with her cheer coach and was supposed to get a parent signature on a form. She decided to forge my signature and turned it in. A few days later, the carbon copy of the form was balled up in the garage. I found it. When I asked Farrell if he remembered it, he said 'no.' We figured out pretty quickly what had happened.

I called her cheer coach and asked her about it. She informed me of the situation and also let me know she would be calling Carli in to explain. Due to the other issues which I was unaware of, she would be asking Carli to step down as Captain until she could prove her leadership.

When Carli was called into the office, she initially tried to lie about it. Then, when faced with proof, she had nothing to say. She just sat there, blankly. Then came the dramatic tears. She was reluctant to step down but did, given the circumstances. It was news to us that Carli was the source of gossip and drama in recent weeks on the cheer team.

Her popularity was going to her head, and the mean girl in her showed its ugly head. Her poor attitude bled into her home life. Her chores started slipping in the house, to the point where she'd whine and cry *not* to have to do her dishes on the nights she was assigned. She sure knew how to cry at the drop of a hat, I will tell you that. She could be quite the drama queen and knew exactly when to turn it on, this I witnessed firsthand.

Up until this point, Carli was involved in both cheer and dance, despite my request to choose one. She swore to us she could handle the load and wouldn't let her grades slip, which she honored. However, since the cheer drama, she decided to and quit the cheer team and focus on dance for her last two years in highschool.

Carli was a beautiful dancer. I saw her pour into herself when performing. I saw her raw emotion, what she hid from the world came out so elegant as the most graceful form of expression. I was equally as excited to support her dance career because of this.

There was a calm after the cheer storm. Carli was focused on dance, putting together routines, getting to know her dance team, and staying out of trouble. She was turning sixteen soon, and we threw her a birthday party. I took her to get her nails done and got her a cute mermaid style dress to go with her theme. We cleared out the downstairs area, set up music, and got her a cake, and she invited her close friends and sisters to celebrate. She had a great day being the center of attention, showing her friends her home and introducing them to her family. She was proud that day, probably the proudest I'd seen her since being here. I was glad to do it for her. We were proud of her for keeping her grades up and committing to dance. Despite the teen and mom and daughter stuff she gave us, she wasn't that bad, certainly no match for anything I hadn't already seen. I think we're going to be just fine.

Soon after her party she came to us and asked if she could go on a date with a guy from the football team. A mother's favorite request. We sat her down and explained to her what dating looked like in this house. This meant that he had to come here to meet us and have her home at the time we wanted. And because he drove, no leaving school without our permission.

Gregory was her age and super sweet but I was no fool. He became her boyfriend that summer. We allowed him to come to the house to pick her up to take her out. We let her go to his home, and we even spoke to his parents. Everything seemed to line up accordingly, and they dated that summer into her junior year.

I liked this guy for her. Caucasian, tall, and a football player. He came from a good family, wholesome. He was already being scouted out by a few colleges. Everything seemed cool between the two until that one day, I asked her to clean the bathroom, and she conveniently forgot and skated off to dance practice.

I cleaned the bathroom that day, it wasn't a big deal to me, and I loved cleaning. I blasted Mary J. Blige and my most recent favorite, Tamar Braxton. I got my cleaning dress on and got my house together. That morning I was on a roll, my energy was high, and things were moving nicely. Last spot: the kids' bathroom. The dreaded teen bathroom. My teenage son and my bonus child occupied this bathroom.

The smell was offensive. The sight, dreadful. In the drawers, old tampons wrapped in toilet tissue pushed to the darkness of the drawer. Piss nearly jumping the ledge of the porcelain throne. Hair was *everywhere*. I ventured under the sink to toss the trash that had been stored there, not too sure why, but nonetheless, I reached back into the abyss of the bathroom sink. I pulled back a wad of napkins, and in it was a small white stick with one blue line. NEGATIVE.

In my hands, ladies and gentlemen, a pregnancy test. A negative one, praise God, but a pregnancy test. I called Farrell, who was at a business training class and alerted him of the crisis ahead. What the hell were we going to do?! We've never dealt with *this* before. I mean, we found Tiffany's Plan B, but she was an adult. This is just all too familiar.

We invited Carli's boyfriend over that next day to have a little chat. Farrell wanted to speak with him, man to man. I wanted Carli to know we knew her secret, a secret that she conveniently hid in the community bathroom.

"Hey, Gregory. We invited you here today to just talk, you know, see how things are going with you two."

"Yes, sir. I understand."

"So, you know we know about the pregnancy test?"

"Yes, Carli told me you guys spoke to her about it."

"Yes, so here's what I want you to do. Take out your phone for me real quick."

Not sure where he was going with this, Gregory and Carli both took out their phones. I sat up and acted as if I knew exactly what direction he was going. My husband was a charismatic businessman. He loved to talk to people and often exuded excitement about teaching others. So we were all in for a lesson.

"Okay, so go on Google, type in 'what's the price or diapers and baby formula,' and let me know what you get."

Gregory, staggering at the answer that he was unprepared to give, "Says about $1,900 per year."

Carli looked down, her favorite place to look in embarrassment.

"Ha. Okay. Now I want to know what hourly wage you would need to make in order to provide *just* the diapers for a baby."

Blank stares from the both of them.

GOT EM.

My husband, I tell ya, the dumbfounded look on each of their faces was priceless. Stark and somewhat lost, Gregory fumbled for the words to follow.

"I'm sorry, sir. I know we shouldn't be doing this. She said she missed her period, so I got scared and got a test. I know we can't have a kid right now. I mean, I still want to go to college."

"Exactly! Here's the thing, Gregory, we get it. What we need you guys to get is the fact that having a baby is *hard* work and will be the responsibility of *you two*, not us or your parents. We want you to be responsible right now, you still have your whole lives ahead of you."

Carli said nothing the entire meeting. She smiled at Gregory with glee when it ended, and they went for ice cream. I took her to get on birth control the next week, I was no fool.

This teen stuff was beginning to weigh on me. I refuse to let them win. Farrell and I did a pretty good job of handling things between the two of them. However, Carli had her fair share of manipulative moments where she tried to play us against each other. A few times, it almost worked. She'd walk around like she had no clue as to why. When her lies caused chaos to ensue within the home, she remained unbothered. I imagined her thinking 'dance puppets, dance.' Luckily, I saw through it every single time.

On top of maintaining my own domain, I, too, was responsible for maintaining my grandmother's affairs. Not her official DPOA, although I was the one in the city who stepped up to help out. Her DPOA and older children, my aunts and uncles were conveniently out of state.

My family and I were the ones who made sure she was comfortable. We prepared meals and took her to doctor appointments. If she fell, Tiffany and I went down there to lift her up. Farrell was on her speed dial and was ready to be called to duty at any given moment. That's just how it went, no questions asked. However, grandma was getting older and required more attention and care. She continued to fall, and the family was really quite naive in understanding the level of care she needed.

We were able to agree on having a nurse come in a few hours a week. The private caregiver would be there to help with medication distribution, meal prep, and companionship. This was perfect, especially in the months my live-in uncle went to jail.

It all became so stressful, stress that I was unable to express because there was no one else. Who else was going to do it? My grandmother called me daily. She spoke of the daily stresses that were placed on her by my aunts and uncles. I had to be there for her, the way my mother would have been, had she been alive.

In the midst of all of these new dynamics in my life, my own health was suffering. My blood pressure continued to rise, and I had no idea how to control it. My daughter, bless her heart, was the health buff in the family since my mother passed and did her best with helping me monitor it. However, it was not going down. The underlying stress was eating away at me; although, my sleep had been uninterrupted and peaceful like always.

I maintained I had to be strong enough not to let this girl take me down. Carli was testing my patience in every way. And then, we'd have a moment where she'd be vulnerable and sweet. We'd talk about her mom, and she'd smile. I'd see flashes of my aunt and remembered why I was doing this. That's one thing she and all the girls could always count on, my door was always open.

We did things as a family: celebrate a few Easters, Fourth of July BBQs, pool days, beach days. We did it all. I was always intentional about getting the kids out on the weekends. I enjoyed seeing the world through their eyes. Farrell and Drew had their bonding time. Farrell was the official spider killer for Carli. She and I had our bonding time as well. Our family dynamics seemed to be running as smoothly as could be given the changes we experienced.

Having a present father figure was something that she always seemed to appreciate. Carli loved sharing goofy jokes with Farrell while he was in the kitchen cooking. She and Drew would just sit there and take turns making him laugh, telling him stories, sharing their lives with him.

The two of them bickered at times as siblings, and I loved it. The love had always been real. She did not play about her baby cousin Drew.

Now, if we could only get these chores under control. It was pretty simple at this point. Carli had to clean the kitchen three days a week. This included dishes (Yes, pots and pans too. Imagine that!), wiping the counters, and sweeping. One of which she forgot at least once a week. Often she ignored the kitchen entirely and was forced to get up in the morning to do it. An agreement that became *her* go-to when she was too tired to clean the night before.

On those mornings, I would wake her up to do her chores, and she fought me every single time. She started with whining and whimpering. When that didn't work, she went into full-blown tears and tantrum mode just to avoid her responsibilities. I caved in the first two times she did it. Then I saw the pattern and quickly got hip and learned to ignore her, turn her light on and walk out of her room. Five in the morning was no time to be negotiating what should have been done last night. That's one thing she was great at, crying and throwing an emotional fit. I saw her do it on the phone with Gregory, and it's pretty crazy how she could transform. I guess that's what makes her dancing so artistic.

We got the call in the evening that my grandmother was quickly declining. Transitioning, they said. The hospice nurses had been out and confirmed that she was, in fact, in her last days. We made it through the summer to August, and she was declining rapidly. Almost too quickly for everyone to make it to see her and say their goodbyes.

Tiffany and I cleaned her up and put her purple satin pajamas on. A Chinese print button-down, and of course, she had slippers to match. Slippers we both knew her tiny little feet would never occupy again.

Allowing the emotions to come, we continued to make her presentable for visitors. She was unresponsive at this point. Grandma was able to open her eyes and respond via touch the first day. By the second day, a little less but more family surrounded her and catered to her in their own unique ways. The cousins came together and were the support system for the ones grieving their mother. Mostly we laughed. We shared stories of mommy, grandma, and great-grandma. We reveled at all of the old family pictures she had displayed in her hallway.

Her apartment was a small two-bedroom upstairs unit that looked like something straight out of HGTV. She'd been there at least twenty-five years, and the place looked immaculate. Her space was designed with the finest Goodwill repurposed furniture and décor. Her home was indeed her personal sanctuary and was a true reflection of her style, her character, and her heart. Chinese curvature carved into designs placed perfectly on her floor-length bookshelf. Jade elephants pranced across the top of the shelf, led by a golden chariot. White lights shadowed from behind, giving the most romantic ambiance of her Chinese dream. An unused, rustic gold tea set sat on the table. Beside it was a cup with tiny pieces of fake sugar. 'Where on earth did she find this,' we all wondered. Her Bible sat open to the book of Psalm. Mirrors ran the length of the walls behind the couches. A small place with great character. So relevant for our Grandmother. I always asked her if one of us won the lottery would she want to move to a home. Her answer had always been the same, followed by a laugh as if she were tickled pink. "I'm just fine where I am."

She was just that. Even in her last days, she was perfectly fine and content. The eight of her ten children, grandchildren and great-grands gathered in her tiny apartment over a few days to say their goodbyes. We all kissed her sweet forehead and told her how much we loved her. The siblings, as wild and crazy as they were, they came together for their mother. The cousins looked out for the siblings and younger generations, and we all got along. We meshed the way she would have wanted, the way she needed, and ultimately the way grandma deserved being the sweet soul she was.

She passed just a few days shy of her birthday, not like she would have cared; she was a longtime Jehovah's Witness and never celebrated her birthday. The family felt broken. We all felt her presence leave this earth, but we comforted each other the way we all knew how: laughter! It was truly our thing and got us through a lot of the sadness and kept a lot of us from feeling angry and bitter about her passing.

In the next few days, the older siblings got together to create her obituary. We gathered pictures from her picture wall and put together a beautiful arrangement of photos and highlights from her life. Tiffany, the writer in the family, became our official obituary poem writer. She wrote a piece for her great grandmother just as she did for her Great Aunt Cara and Grandma Sharon. We used a picture of Grandma Bella Marie from when she was healthy and vibrant. She smiled so brightly in nearly all of her old photos. There was one in particular of her in her brown suit, short tapered wig, and beautiful background that just so happened to be her very own bedroom. This specific picture she seemed alive and energetic, radiance pulsating through her award-winning smile.

We held her service at her local Kingdom Hall. The women of the family decided to honor her by picking one of her fabulous hats from her colorful collection. Each of us matched our hats with our outfits. When we walked into the Kingdom Hall, we sure did turn heads like we knew we would. Her Witness brothers and sisters were so impressed and complimentary in how we decided to honor Ms. Bella Marie. Her very own hat ladies here to honor her legacy and carry the torch of love and laughter as we embraced this world without her.

In the true fashion of this family, we made no immediate plans after the funeral. With love being so high, we didn't want to part, so Farrell and I opened up our home to the family to come and hang. We listened to music and hosted it pot luck style so we could all be together. We put that gathering together so fast and effectively. Everyone picked up something or contributed in some way. There, in my home under the infamous wedding picture in our living room, sat three poster-size photos in order of passing. From left to right: my mother Sharon, who passed May 2011, my Aunt Cara, who passed August 2011, and lastly, Grandma Bella Marie, who passed just recently. There they all sat, watching over us. My grandmother's sisters were there as well. They were the matriarchs of us all now. They love seeing the family dance around and enjoy each other. With plenty of food, wine, and Farrell on the ones and twos, we celebrated Ms. Bella Marie. We danced to old school songs, shared old stories, caught up, and, most of all, laughed. After all, it was our thing.

Dear Jehovah,
Life is getting hard, but I know you are strengthening me. I miss my grandmother. I pray the family continues to stick together. Thank you for the time we spent with our grandmother. I pray that we can remember her spirit and her love on our hardest days. Jehovah I pray I can do a good job with Carli, I have been under a lot of stress, but I know it is not in vain. I have been called to this for a reason, and I accept the call. I pray for protection over my family.
In Jesus' name, we pray. Amen.
Mirabel

Dear Mommy,

A lot has changed in a year. I found a great guy, Gregory. You would love him. He reminds me so much of daddy! Especially his jokes! Mirabel and Farrell have been great with letting me do things when I ask. I hate doing chores, though. I guess not much has changed, huh. LOL. I really miss you, Mom, but I know you would be proud of me because I'm actually happy. I have friends, and I'm popular at school. I was one of the best cheerleaders, but now my focus is on dance. I sometimes imagine you are watching me when I dance. Kinda creepy, I know, but it helps me go deeper, and I know that you are proud. My sisters are annoying at times, but that's just them, I guess. I like being the big sis around the house. Drew and I are still so close. I just wanted to update you because I know Grandma Marie is on her way up there, so I wanted to update you first. I love you, Mommy!
Your Car Car

To my family,
I'm sorry I had to leave this earth, but I have instilled in you exactly what you need to move through this crazy life. I have instilled in you the love of our beloved Jehovah God and his beautiful masterpieces. I have taught you forgiveness and strength through nothing but love. Lead with this at all times, my children. Your brothers and sisters, their children, and their children that is my legacy—protect, honor, and nurture it. It is part of every single one of you, it is us. We share it in the gleam of our smiles, the soft beat of an aching heart, we are magic because we were created in the likeness of the divine. I love you, my children. It is my time, and it is your time to transform what I've done for us into something that can last the true test of time. Until we meet again in the new system.
I love you
Bella Marie

Chapter 14: Year Five

MIRABEL

The funeral was beautiful. The after-party was exactly what we needed. My grandmother's sisters sat in awe of how similar we were. How much we were all *just* like the lady we just laid to rest. That despite what sadness we still felt, we were able to celebrate her in a way that commemorated a woman who led with love her entire life. We danced all night long. Farrell kept us guessing with old school songs and dances that deemed us "old fogies" by our younger generation of cousins. We needed this time together. I was glad our home was the place we could gather. Like times before, our family drama took a backseat to the importance of coming together in a time of need. That's what we were good at.

The family continued to stay close after grandma's passing. My uncle and I didn't know what to do with ourselves. All we knew was how to care for grandma. He lived with her full time when he wasn't in jail and loved the hell out of her.

He called me several times a day just to say 'hi,' check-in, be silly, and find his strength. I embraced his calls because only the two of us knew what it was like to see grandma decline as rapidly as she did. The two of us bonded in ways that only we could understand. 'Trauma bonds' I think they call them. Either way, we were bonded and branded for life for honoring my grandmother and his mother in her last days.

Sad to say, I couldn't say the same for most of my aunts and uncles. Many went on with their lives shortly after the service. Some did their own grieving in ways that many of us could not understand. Most became distant. It was almost as if they were relieved that she was gone. The family dynamics changed slightly. Still, the core group here in California stayed close, which we all loved and basked in every chance we could get.

As the fall days quickly turned to winter, the fall leaves escaped the trees, much like the happiness that eluded my spirit. With Christmas approaching, we were doing our annual "Cousins Christmas" however, life just seems so heavy right now.

Carli's attitude was so wishy-washy. She and Gregory were off and on. This teen love stuff was quite dramatic. Other than being an ear and shoulder, I really had to let her figure it out. She opened up to me, but as of late, it became less and less. It was no coincidence that her eighteenth birthday was roughly eight months away. She'd checked out mentally, and it showed.

The last few times she came home from her sisters, she had a suspicious case of food poisoning. Alana was the one who made sure to explain for her upon bringing her home. Food poisoning, twice in a month. Well, what the hell was she eating? Coincidentally those both times she came back from her sisters, her hair also wreaked of alcohol. Go figure. I was aware there were fewer rules when she was with her sisters. I was also aware that they often had a lot of friends over, and that's fine because that's what they choose to do. They didn't understand that Carli was heavily influenced by this lifestyle of leisure and fun.

I was afraid it was rubbing off on her in more ways than one. Carli was reluctant to drive as a seventeen-year-old. Tiffany was *ready* at sixteen. Carli, on the other hand, was taking her sweet time. We'd gotten her the driver's ed book and later found it ripped up under her bed. We downloaded the book online for her to sit and read, and she ended up doing less and less of the reading.

Working came secondary to her busy dance schedule. Most seniors her age did both or at least worked weekends. We also encouraged this, so she could know how great it felt to have her own money for the many McDonald's runs she requested. We took her around to collect job applications. We even coached her on what to say and how to conduct herself when asking for the application. We helped her fill them out only to find them piled on the kitchen table. I couldn't win. I don't know what teen loved to eat and shop but didn't want their own money. She was able to quietly finesse cash out of her sister Alana. She had always been good at that since their mom passed. Alana was her go-to for the nurturing the compassion and the emotional response. Brianna was a lot tougher and not easily impressed with her theatrics.

Nonetheless, her sisters continue to let her get away with far more than we would even allow. They covered up for her in true sister fashion. The difference here was that Carli was a minor, and *we* were responsible for her at all times.

The environment they created for her on the weekends she visited was much like, a weekend at dad's. It's the best time ever! You get to eat whatever, watch whatever, stay out late, etc. And yet, there were many weekends she didn't come home hungover. Sometimes she'd return starving and saying she hadn't really eaten with them all weekend. She would say money was tight for them, and she'd scarf down our traditional Sunday dinner complete with a dessert.

I never took to heart the issues Carli and I began to have as she morphed into adulthood. I knew things would get rocky. I experienced this twice already with Tiffany and my bonus daughter Iman. Between the two of them, I could handle anything. Carli was no different. She was actually a typical teen trying to get away with lying and was hardly successful. I could look right at her and know she was lying before she opened her mouth. Then came the tears and dramatization of "oh shit, she caught me." I knew this girl too well, and she hated it. She hated that she couldn't manipulate me like she did her sisters and those little boys around her school. She knew that I didn't fall for her sweet smile and innocent voice.

As of late, I figured out that she spent a lot of time either trying to cover something up, conjure up some drama, or arguing with her boyfriend so the whole house could hear. Our relationship continued to become strained. Sometimes I felt like she hated me. Eh, well, that meant I was doing what needed to be done as the maternal figure in her life.

She's tried to pit Farrell and me against one another. We've argued about things regarding the kids many times. I would tell her, 'no.' She would then ask him. And he would say 'yes' before we got a chance to talk, so we were left to argue it out. We'd been there a couple of times actually, left to pick up the pieces of another one of Carli's lies.

Now she's a Gemini, so not every day is chaotic and drama-filled. In the mornings before Farrell took them to school, she'd come in to greet me and the daycare kids with a funny joke or story, which I do enjoy. She and Drew had their own handshake and weird cousin bond that I loved. Tiffany helped manage her hair by cutting and straightening it from time to time. She was always so happy to show the family a new dance move or routine when we had our gatherings. Typical teen, like I said, so I didn't take any of it to heart. I was also trying not to allow her to take me out, so I continued to pray.

I prayed mostly for peace and guidance in all of this. I prayed I was doing right by Carli, by my family and by myself. My spirit wondered if to let her go with her sisters when she graduated. After all, the initial agreement was for five years. At this point, it was time for them to show her the power of sisterhood.

Farrell and I celebrated our fifteenth anniversary at the start of the new year. Tiffany made us the best gift. She asked the family near and far to send in videos of them wishing us a happy fifteen years. She then presented it to us before we all went to dinner. I cried when the video panned to Carli's video. I'm not sure why the emotion came out. In her video, I saw my aunt, I saw my promise, and I saw a young lady that had grown so much in the last five years.

Carli's eighteenth birthday was roughly six months away. Farrell and I decided that it would be best for her to transition to living with her sisters once she graduated. She loved the idea when we brought it up to her. She understood that we would do this for five years, and we would all decide. For me, at that point, I knew she would be happiest becoming a young woman with her sisters. This was where they'd step in and take the torch. With Carli turning eighteen and on her way to college, if she chose, she could work and live with her sisters. We could then redirect our family dynamics back to cousins and continue our version of happily ever after.

Of course, we would still be there for her. We planned to be a resource for her in any way, much like a parent would. However, I knew her living here as an eighteen-year-old was not going to work. There were still rules in my home, even for eighteen-year-olds. Tiffany had a curfew at eighteen and had specific rules she needed to respect to live here, rules she was happy to oblige to knowing the alternative. I was due for a break, given my own health concerns these last few years. Also, attention needed to be placed on Drew, who was now in high school. I had done my best and felt free to release myself from the job of being Carli's parent.

When we asked Alana and Brianna to come over to discuss this, they were more than happy. With Carli present, we started by reminding them of the original agreement. The time was approaching for things to shift in another direction. Carli was so excited to reveal she'd be coming to live with them in their condo, much closer to her friends and the freedom she sought. She was met with a sinister look from Brianna. A look of anxiety permanently pierced Alana's face.

"Look, Carli. You better get your shit together. That means you need to get a job. If you can't pay rent, I will kick you out," Brianna fired off. "And you better not think you are coming with this attitude either. I've heard how you've been so disrespectful to Mirabel and Farrell. I should slap you for that, like come on, they take great care of you."

Carli stared blankly into the distance.

Alana chimed in. "Well, Carli, what Brianna means is we obviously want you to come live with us, but we both have work and school and our boyfriends. We only have our two-bedroom, so it's going to be tight, so we need you to pull your weight. Okay, Carli-Bear?"

"Stop babying her. She better not come to our house with bullshit. I'm not playing. You'll be *out!*"

Farrell and I tried to shift the conversation to something a bit more positive. We could see the immediate stress of what was to come settling into both of their spirits. Carli clearly had a different idea of what was going to happen when she moved in. My guess was she thought it was going to be like it was on the weekends. Carli got a rude awakening as her precious sisters, who often had a hard time telling her no, just told her that she will be responsible for herself and had to work. Those were two concepts I struggled to get her to grasp as of late. This was why she needed her sisters; they could give her the unapologetic kick in the ass she needed to jump-start her life.

Now that everyone was on board with the plans for the next few months, I could rest just a little easier. Alana and Briana prepped their condo for her arrival. Farrell and I helped Carli to get established at the community college here in town. We attempted the job application process and really helped to set her up to be self-sufficient. We even considered getting her a car for graduation. Something small and reliable, so that was less for her sisters to worry about. However, due to her recent bouts of irresponsibility and blatant disrespect, we decided against it. Instead, we planned to send her off with money and resources to aid her in adulthood.

All of this planning for her future also coincided with a teen girl's most favorite time of year: senior prom! In true jock fashion, Gregory asked her to prom by utilizing his teammates. She was smitten and so excited to get dressed up like a princess.

Alana called early in the morning to ask if we could talk about the arrangements when she brought Carli's prom shoes. Unsure of where she's going with this, I accepted the invitation. After all, we weren't taking Carli's dress in to be altered until later, and she needed the shoes, so it worked out.

"Hey, Mirabel. Me and Brianna talked to Sherry, and she thinks having Carli live with us in our condo would be a liability. So we were thinking you and Farrell can think it over and consider letting Carli stay here."

Sherry was Alana's boyfriend's mother. The family was well off. When Cara passed away, she stepped up and took the girls under her wing. In the last few years, she purchased the condo they now lived in to help give them stability.

"Well, Alana, I'm not sure why you are allowing Sherry to speak about your *sister* in that manner, calling her a liability. As far as I'm concerned, this is a *family* matter. That is your *sister*."

"I know, but I don't want to go against her. We can't lose our place, and we can't afford just to take care of Carli, either."

"Your sister needs you right now, that's the bottom line. Sherry is just going to have to understand. Farrell and I have a plan to help her get situated. We're not going to just dump her on you. We will be right here if she gets out of hand or anything like that. You guys will be fine. I'm sure of it."

Alana sat there dumbfounded as Carli walked up the stairs. Twenty minutes before she was excited for prom. She heard everything. Upon seeing Carli, Alana jumped up and gave her a hug and rushed out the door explaining she had an errand to get to for Sherry.

We went on with our day of prom shopping and a lunch date. Carli's mood eventually lightened, and we never spoke about what she heard. I knew deep down she was hurting from hearing her sisters' inability and unwillingness to take her in.

The day of the prom was a gorgeous one. We found a beautiful Tiffany blue gown with a sweetheart neckline. It also had jewels dancing along the border of the breast line. The dress was long, and it flowed beautifully off of her thin figure. Her hair was done in an updo with curly tendrils framing her face. We went to M.A.C. for makeup because, apparently, that's what *everyone* does. Her shoes looked pretty similar to Cinderella's glass slipper. She looked flawless. And her smile? Her smile set the entire look off. The whole day was about her and Gregory. He did a fantastic job of making her his princess for the night despite the hiccups they faced as of late.

Our family gathered with the other prom couples to take pictures. Alana and Brianna came to participate. They were so happy and proud to see their baby sis grow into such a beautiful young lady. The day was perfect.

With just one month left for the senior class, Carli was definitely showing signs of the senior blues. She broke up with Gregory two weeks after prom and was not the same since. She was far quieter. She saught far more attention on social media and had dark energy about her.

Ah, yes, she was about to be eighteen and thought she was grown. I remembered this phase. At this point, I had to ignore when Carli purposely tried to get under my skin. I knew as well as she did that our time in this mother-daughter phase was coming to an end. In just a few more weeks, we would pack up her items, watch her walk across that stage, shout for our Carli-Bear, and prepare the transition to womanhood and sisterhood.

During this time, Carli and I bonded as I helped her go through her things. Together we determined what she would take, what stayed, and what would go in the trash. I loved cleaning and organizing, so this was more like fun for me. We laughed together as we found old pictures of her and Drew at one of his birthday parties from when they were young. She tried on her old cheer costume for shits and giggles. We shared a moment when she came across her mother's obituary. Wow, the very moments that brought us to *this* moment. How chilling. She packed it away in the keepsake pile, and we continued on through the mess she called a room.

Graduation was approaching, and the plans were set. The night of graduation, Carli, Alana, Brianna, Tiffany, Drew, Tammy, myself, and Farrell went out for dinner. The Saturday following her graduation, the family gathered at the house for my famous chicken and waffles and my honey cake that Carli requested to celebrate her graduating. This meal would be more of a celebratory meal for all of us because we made it. This would be the best batch of homemade chicken and waffles I ever made. I put my heart in *everything* I did, an inevitable fact of my life.

Dear Jehovah,

Thank you for getting Carli this far. Thank you for getting us this far. I pray you guide her as she moves into this new phase of life. Keep her protected, honest, and humbled. I ask that you soften her spirit and allow her to shine the way you intend for her life. I pray protection and peace for her sisters. I pray they can guide her and be there for her only the way a sister knows how to. Thank you for blessing this journey and keeping us alive and well and connected through the spirit of you. Thank you, Jehovah, for your mercy on our lives. We did it, and it is because of you.

In Jesus' name, we pray. Amen.

Mirabel

Dear Mommy,

I'm graduating in a few days, and I can't wait. My friends and I are going to take some cool grad pics. LOL.

Gregory and I broke up. I'm graduating, and he isn't this year. I just need to be single right now to explore, and we keep arguing, so we just said we're done.

I think he is talking to someone else, which I hate. I don't like anyone right now. Well, one guy, he's nineteen! He graduated last year. He never talked to me before, but now he started talking to me on Twitter. He's really cute!

I'm moving in with my sisters soon. I was super excited to go and just be free with them like they did when they were my age. But, it's going to suck because they want me to pay bills. My plan is to go to community college, I think. I really don't want to. I don't know what I want to do. I wish I could stay here, but I know I'm not going to follow the rules when I'm eighteen. I really don't know how to ask if I can stay. I thought my sisters would be more excited to have me. I'm starting to feel a little lost. Life seems so big and me so small right now. I wish you were here to make me laugh. I can't wait to turn eighteen, to be an adult! I love you, Mom. Please visit me in my dreams soon.

Carli

Chapter 15: Turning Eighteen

MIRABEL

"The big day is approaching, Carli. What are you going to do?" Drew asked Carli on the way to school. "I don't know yet. Probably something fun with my sisters!" she said excitedly.

That evening I got a call from Brianna, who asked if we had any plans for Carli's birthday. I told her that we were going to let Carli decide what she wanted to do. If it worked out that we all do something as a family, then we'd go from there. They wanted to take Carli to get her belly button pierced and matching sister tattoos.

What was up with these teens wanting to mutilate their bodies? Tiffany was the same way; she rushed to get her belly button pierced when she turned eighteen. I don't get it. I'd never been into piercings, aside from my nose. Tattoos? Never. Would you put a bumper sticker on a Bentley? I digress.

I agreed to let them have her this weekend so they could take her to do fun sister stuff. Brianna said Carli *must* get her belly pierced, given that she had the flattest stomach of all the ladies in the family. Again, I don't get it, but it was not for me to get. This was for them to bond as sisters.

When Carli got home from school, she asked if I could take her to Ross to find a birthday outfit.

"You excited about your birthday?" I asked as we gathered into the car.

"I'm so happy. My sisters are going to go all out. I can't wait! I told Alana I want to do a shopping spree too and she said okay! This is going to be the best birthday ever!"

"I'm glad you're excited! I'll cook your favorite meal, so when you come home, you'll have something to eat to complete your day. What do you want?"

Turning slowly to look at me, her face lively and overjoyed. "Chicken and waffles!"

POST BIRTHDAY BLUES

She walked into the house and went straight downstairs to her room. She greeted us with a level of despair in her spirit that led Farrell, Drew, and me to believe her birthday plans did not turn out the way she hoped. Drew eventually made his way downstairs to talk to her and make sure she was okay.

"Hey, Car. Can I come in?" He asked, standing outside her room.

She mumbled from under the covers, "Sure."

"Hey. Is everything okay? You seem down. How was it at your sisters'?"

"We didn't do shit." She declared.

"Those bitches didn't even have money to do anything. Said I would have to wait for another weekend!"

"Oh, wow. Did you do *anything* for your birthday?"

"They had their friends over Friday night, which was fun. I guess. Wasn't really for me but we had fun. Saturday, they were hungover and broke, so I went and hung out with friends at the movies."

"Oh, wow. That's crazy."

"So no one cares about my birthday. Your mom and dad didn't even do anything. This sucks. My life sucks."

Slowly retreating out of her room and out of the garage, Drew walked upstairs and came to Farrell and me to let us know how she was doing.

"Mom, Carli is sad. She thinks no one cares about her eighteenth birthday. We gotta do something."

"Drew, I am making her chicken in waffles tonight, and I even baked her a cake! She said she had all of these fun plans with her sisters. What happened?"

"Mom, she's downstairs, almost crying. Her sisters didn't do what they said, there was no tattoo and no piercing. She thinks no one cares about her."

"I'll go down and talk to her."

"Carli, it's Mirabel can I come in?"

I opened her squeaky room door. She shuffled on the bed to make room. I walked over the pile of clothes in the middle of the floor. I was unsure what that stench was, but now wasn't the time to get on her about her room. I opened the curtains to let some sun in. On her mantel, there were glasses and cups. The window sill and everywhere had hairballs. Not saying I'm OCD about cleaning or organization, but this mess was ridiculous.

"Carli, is everything okay?"

Struggling through her steady stream of tears, "No one cares about me. My sisters did nothing for my birthday. I miss my mom."

"Carli, baby, we didn't do anything else because you had a plan with your sisters. I did make your favorite meal and even baked you a cake with confetti frosting. Your favorite!"

Smiling and excited, "You did?!"

"Yes, we were planning on having dinner together when Tiffany gets home. Tammy will be over too! We also got you a gift card so you can do that shopping spree you've been wanting."

Smiling and crawling out from under her self-made barricade, she gave me a hug. We went upstairs together to watch our family's favorite show: *The Family Feud*. We laughed, ate, and had cake for her eighteenth birthday. She was content and ready for her last days as a senior.

JUNE 3

We made it. Today was the last day for the senior class. Carli got out earlier than Drew, being that he was an underclassman. Drew asked if he could walk home rather than get picked up by Farrell after school let out. He and his friends were going to go hang out at this burger place near our home. Carli then asked if she too could walk home. She wanted to stay for a bit and say her goodbyes to her fellow classmates. We agreed since she'd walked home before. All I asked was that she checked in to let me know she was good.

It had been an hour since Carli got out of school. I hadn't heard anything from her. That wasn't unusual. She probably got caught up in the last day's festivities.

Forty-five minutes later, I picked up my phone to call Farrell to see if he'd heard from her. At this time in came a call from Ms. Carli.

"Hey, Mirabel."

"Hey, Carli. You okay? Where are you?"

"Still at the school. Can I walk to the Mexican restaurant and get a burrito?"

Unsure of why she sounded different, almost rushing me off the phone. My suspicions grew. Frankly, because she was moving to her sisters this weekend, I didn't have the energy even to question this eighteen-year-old any further.

"Sure. I don't care, Carli. Come home after."

"Okay," and she hung up the phone.

That was the last time we heard from Carli that day. Something did not sit right with me, but I gave her the benefit of the doubt. Hours passed. I put the word out to her sisters that if they heard from her to make her go to their house. I could not look at her right now.

They were pissed. Knowing that she was about to be their responsibility while acting out in such an outlandish fashion. They agreed to have her come there if she contacted them. She hadn't contacted anyone at this point. Our worry was growing. Finally, around 5 PM, I called her phone. She answered in a low and sinister tone.

"Hello."

"Carli, where are you? You went to get a burrito and never came home. WHERE ARE YOU?!"

"I'm at the mall with a friend."

"Who told you you could go to the mall? You only asked to go for a burrito and never came home after school."

"Well, you said you didn't care."

"I SAID I DIDN'T CARE ABOUT YOU GOING TO THE MEXICAN RESTAURANT! GET HOME!"

"I'm eighteen. I'll come back when I'm ready. I'm out right now. I don't know when I'll be back."

Later that day, Carli phoned her sister Alana, the one she could finesse. With graduation just a day away, we are all unsure of what the hell was going on. We planned to attend her graduation, have a nice family dinner, and get her moved. Yet our graduate was on her final act—a disappearing act.

"Alana, it's me, Carli."

"What the hell, Carli. You need to get your ass back to Mirabel and Farrell's *now*."

"Mirabel kicked me out. I need a ride. She said I could go to the mall and is flipping out on me for no reason."

"Carli, stop lying! We spoke to Mirabel, and no, she did not! You left for school this morning and haven't been back since. Get your ass home!"

"Alana, but she did. She told me never to come back."

"Carli, you owe Mirabel and Farrell an apology. After all they've done for you. How dare you! Get off my phone *right* now and call Mirabel. I will come get you wherever you are. We have to get you ready for graduation, what in the actual fuck!"

"FUCK YOU, ALANA!" And she hung up on her sister.

Alana and Brianna were in contact with us when she stopped answering their calls. They were sure they would frighten her enough to bring her back, but we all know the bully tactic never works.

The next day Carli texted me after being gone overnight. She asked when she could come back to our house. Nearly confused, I asked where she was. She decided to call Farrell as speaking to me gave her anxiety. I sure could say the same. I let Farrell know she would be calling.

Carli hung up the phone and called Farrell.

"Hello."

"Hey, Farrell. It's Carli."

"Hey. You okay?"

"Yea."

"Okay. Good. Glad to hear that. Why don't you come home and we'll deal with this stuff later. Let's get you ready for graduation. You made it this far. Don't quit now."

"I don't want to come back there. Can I come to get my stuff? Mirabel makes me uncomfortable."

Her things were already packed and ready since she was going to be moving with her sisters this weekend. We shared a nice bond while cleaning and organizing everything. How have *I* made her uncomfortable? We sang and danced around to different jams. Seriously, what the hell is going on?

Farrell confused as hell, "Carli what are you talking about?! Look, just come home and we'll handle this later. Let's go get your diploma, girl!"

"If I come there, I'm coming to get my things."

"Okay, Carli. I'm still confused as to why you won't come here. So why don't you go ahead and go to your sisters, they are expecting you."

Click.

An hour later, a silver jeep crept slow and steady up our driveway. In the driver's seat sat Carli's friend Destiny. There was also some girl who I'd never seen before. Carli looked like she had a long night. She was dressed in the same clothes she left for school in the day prior. She had bags under her eyes and the apparent stench of alcohol seeping through her pores. Is *this* is the young lady I raised for the last five years? Can't be.

I was confused, but I spoke directly. There was an undertone of emotional exhaustion, but I mustered up the courage to calmly ask her right there in front of her friends, "Carli, what are you doing?"

"Hi, Mirabel!" Destiny cheerfully chimed in to fill the awkward space between two cousins—or were we still parent-child? Adult to adult?

Woman to woman.

"I'm getting my stuff." She said, so matter of factly.

Carli gathered her items that were already packed. Destiny asked me about the daycare. This was all happening so fast. I was so confused yet composed enough to speak to her with respect and calmness because number one I was at work. Two, this girl wouldn't have me catch a case. So, calm, cool, and collective it was.

She walked into the daycare and placed her high school graduation tickets on the counter.

I reached down and hand them back to her.

"Um, Carli, I won't be going to your graduation. Everyone else is still going to go. All of a sudden, you're not comfortable with me?" I awaited her answer. She shuffled to avoid meeting my gaze.

"No, no, I am not comfortable with you," soft and gentle, she let those words slide through her teeth like a spotless string of floss. Teeth that *we* spent thousands of dollars on perfecting with braces and dental hygiene.

My heart sank, but I showed no reaction. Carli's friends stood there awkwardly, shifting their gaze from left to right, unsure of how to react. What was coming next? How serious Carli was about what she just said?

"Okay, Carli. Okay."

By this time, Farrell was on his way home. Matter fact, he came up the driveway on her way out. Carli was aware of this as he was on the phone with me when this conversation began. Carli and her crew rushed to load up Destiny's car to speed off down the driveway and never look back.

I phoned her sisters and let them know what just happened. I also told them that I was in the middle of working and couldn't adequately deal with this the way I would if I were not.

"Carli came here with her friends just now and got her stuff. Farrell wasn't here. He was on his way; she knew that and left anyway. I'm working; she knew I couldn't do anything to stop her. Can you guys talk to her or something? I don't know what to do at this point."

Brianna, unable to fully contain herself, "Oh, wow. Mirabel, she's so fucking stupid! I'm so pissed at her! What is wrong with her? I'm going to make her apologize! I'm going to call her and call you back."

Five minutes later, my phone rang.

"I just yelled at her and told her she better call you guys and apologize, or *we're* not going to her graduation. This is crazy. She's acting like a little bitch. You guys have done so much. I'm so sorry."

"You don't have to apologize, and neither does she. She feels how she feels. She'll calm down and come around. And this is teen stuff she's going through, it's going to pass. I don't think you should've told her that you guys won't go. She needs you right now. It's important that you go."

"Fine, we'll still go. I'll see if she'll answer my calls. I cussed her out pretty bad. Ha!"

Brianna tried to call Carli twenty-seven times. She also sent fourteen text messages before she stopped. Carli was done with them after her exchange with Brianna. I heard things got intense on both ends.

Next thing we know, Drew revealed that a friend of his was inquiring about his cousin Carli selling her graduation tickets on Twitter. He wanted to buy a few.

WOW.

So even if her sisters wanted to go see their baby sister walk the stage, they would have to find tickets to do so. Would they catch her before she sold them all? This was probably the craziest situation we'd been in in a long time, and everyone was looking to me for answers. My answer remained the same: leave her be. She will come back. The more we harassed her, the more rebellious she was going to be. "Clearly, we ain't seen nothing yet, and this girl was just getting started. Don't text and don't call, unless they are 'we love you and miss you' texts. She will eventually need a hot meal, a hot shower, or a hot kick in the ass. And when she does, she'll venture home."

Not one family member made it to Carli's graduation that June. Her graduation day: a day we all looked forward to because of the struggles we all faced transitioning into what would become *this* moment. Carli attended and posted one picture on her Twitter page that Drew let us see. She looked dark as in her energy. Her aura seemed distant. That was not the girl who left out of here just a few days ago asking for permission to get a burrito. What just happened here?

Dear Jehovah,

What a day! First, thank you for keeping me calm and protected today. Only you know what could have gone down had I not been in your grace, so thank you. I would like to pray for Carli's safety and for her spirit. I pray you be the one to reach her and bring her home to family when she is ready. I pray the family can stick together and help Carli through this next challenging phase of life. I pray for her sisters that they have patience with her and understanding of who she really is. I pray they can bond in this new phase. Jehovah, I pray you protect my family and continue to guide our footsteps along the path of your will.

In Jesus' name, we pray. Amen.

Mirabel

Chapter 16: While She's Away

MIRABEL

The following week we celebrated Drew's birthday. It was nice to focus on something and someone else for a change. He could always make us laugh. As a family, Carli included, we often had a great time together.

During this time, no one had been in contact with Carli. However, her Twitter and other social media accounts were alive and *very* active. She never responded to anyone's attempts to reach her there, and after a week, we all stopped trying.

Carli reached out to Drew for his birthday. She said she was staying with a nameless friend. She wanted to get together with him to do something for his birthday. He engaged in the conversation with her, and they laughed and joked like normal. See, she'd be making her way back to her sisters soon.

Because we found out she was selling her graduation tickets on a Twitter account that no one knew about, we were able to keep tabs on her while she was away.

Yolanda, our aunt up north, took it upon herself to zero in on this Twitter account. This info came out in random conversation with my aunts Yolanda and Francis. Now Yolanda didn't mean to tell me this, she slipped up, but I caught it.

What we found was an alter ego of the person we knew and loved. She spoke different—different slang, different twang. Going back over the last year, we saw her wild posts began when she and Gregory started having their major issues. This also correlated with her turning eighteen and moving to her sisters.

 **CARLI CUTEY**
@BearliCar

When I come downstairs, and she asks why I have so much makeup on. Maybe I like to wear this much makeup, you whore. #goodmorning #mamabitch

8:07 PM · January 20

This particular morning she came downstairs ready for school with a face full of makeup. I'm talking heavy dark eyeliner and a smokey eye, dark lipstick, heavy bronzer, and blush. I asked why so much because she was *just* complaining to me about her skin breaking out. But of course, to the outside world, I'm the bad guy.

CARLI CUTEY
@BearliCar

TWO ON!!! Having the best time bumming drinks off hotties!! #turnt #musicfestival #drunkkkkk

11:23 PM · April 16

The night she begged me to go to a music festival, she missed curfew by an hour that day, came straight home and passed out and didn't wake until Sunday evening. What the heck is 'two on' anyways?

CARLI CUTEY
@BearliCar

Sometimes I even believe things in my head that aren't true lol, real shit sometimes I make up my own reality and go with it lmao #dealwithit #geminis

8:32 PM · April 5

Finally, she admitted it. This had always been a challenge for me. I've discovered in the five years I've lived with Carli that when she tells a lie, she will stick with it until the end. She begins to believe her lie, just like she told her sisters I gave her permission to go to the mall when the mall never came up in our conversation.

CARLI CUTEY
@BearliCar

CARLI CUTEY @BearliCar: *I can't wait to turn 18, can't wait to have no rules, can't wait to do ME. #fuckyou #justwaitonit*

3:45 PM · May 8

So, you mean to tell me that two of my aunts *knew* about this account and didn't say anything? They knew *how* I raised my children and *knew* I would not tolerate such behavior or talk online. You mean to tell me that at this stage in my life, as close as we all are, that I didn't deserve respect— that they couldn't tell me what was being said about me online by someone living in my home?

They called me when my own kids posted things online. Iman was number one for posting how she feels online, and family members were always calling me. The difference was my two oldest were grown and can post what they choose—even if I disagreed. But a minor displaying such bratty and ungrateful behavior while out drinking is grounds for a phone call. Its parent code. At least it should be.

Maybe they wanted us to fail all along. How could they know about this Twitter account and what Carli had been doing but not say anything? They came to my home, smiled in my face, and lied that I was doing a great job with her. That was neither here nor there at this point.

If we really want to talk facts, not many of my aunts and uncles even reached out to Carli over the years. Not many checked to see if she needed anything or if she was okay. None of them ever attempted to come to any of her extracurricular activities or performances. Their support only came in the form of a like or comment on Facebook. They said how proud they were of her yet hardly showed up for her the way everyone did for the twins. That's because they knew we had it and did a damn good job, and as long as they could all feel part of their lives, it was all good. Meanwhile, we were actually in the trenches with these girls, and right now, a little support from them now would go a long way.

Yolanda had been in my corner since this all went down. Tiffany updated her as they had their own special bond. Yolanda was quick to call me for the latest scoop. I wish I had more to give her, I really didn't know what happened. Yoland decided to help by making a fake Twitter account and reaching out to Carli. Not sure how effective that would be, and it wasn't my job to convince a very boisterous Yolanda against it.

So, she made one. Initially, Yolanda was talking to Carli as a decoy for reasons only she knew. She harassed Carli daily. Yolanda called Carli a whore, hoe, slut, and every other name in the book. She threatened to punch her in the face. That was Yolanda's go-to threat. We all laughed whenever she said it. This continued until Carli blocked that page.

So, she made another. My aunt was in her early fifties and was on Twitter going at it with her eighteen-year-old niece. What had my life become, Jehovah?

"Yolanda, leave her alone. She will come back when she's ready. She'll have the twins to deal with. She doesn't have to worry about me."

"That little hoe needs to be taught a lesson. No one messes with my niece Mirabel and nephew Farrell! After all, y'all have done for her; she needs to be punched in the face! Haha."

Yolanda always carried the energy of the protector in the family, especially over her nieces. She was the loud one, extremely funny with a temper not to be challenged on the right day.

I laughed because if my aunt was crazy enough to say something like that at her age, she just might be crazy enough to do it.

"Francis told me to continue talking to her to keep the lines of communication open. I will probably do that from my normal page, haha, so she knows it's me. I guess I can come out of hiding!"

"Okay, I guess that makes sense so we can keep tabs on how she is, just be nice, try talking to her, so she'll feel comfortable to come back right now. I'm sure she thinks we all hate her, and that isn't the case."

"Speak for yourself."

A week had gone by, and we are almost to the end of June. It's been about three weeks since the graduation ordeal. I was ready for a new month.

Tiffany was graduating from her esthetician program next week. It felt good to be celebrating again with family despite the circumstance. Yolanda called Tiffany and me with daily updates about Carli. She revealed what they spoke about, what she posted, and if she was well. If Yolanda couldn't reach me, she'd call Tiffany, and they'd vent about this and wonder how it's going to unfold.

"I had a nice chat with Carli. She's starting to open up to me a little more. She is staying with a friend and babysitting another friend's daughter for extra money. I told her that she has some major explaining to do because we are all wondering who this Twitter persona is!"

"Good, I'm glad she's open to talking to you. Just be patient with her. She'll come around."

"Yea and she better have an explanation as to why all this promiscuous behavior! I told her that I became promiscuous after I was violated as a young child, and I never forgave my trespasser. I went after men to get even, so she better have an answer soon because we will want to know what all this behavior is like."

"You shared that with her? What did she say?"

"Yes, my therapist thinks it's good to tell my story, it's healing. She didn't say anything. She just said, 'oh.'"

A few days later, Yolanda phoned to tell me that Carli's Twitter went quiet, and she wasn't answering DMs from any of her decoy pages anymore. Life seemed to go on for a few days, and the dust was settling. I continued planning Tiffany's surprise dinner to celebrate the completion of her program. I arranged for the family and close friends to meet at a local restaurant to celebrate our girl and send her off proper. Tiffany would be moving to Florida in the next few months to open her business and further her studies in the industry. She was ready for a new start, and this dinner was a small token to show her we cared.

Dear Jehovah
Thank you for getting us all this far in this journey. I know your grace has not left us. I pray for Carli at this time. I pray you soften her heart and bring her home safe and sound, well to her sisters, but you know what I mean. I thank you for having a family that steps up when needed, I pray our love continues to stand the test of time. I pray my mother and grandmother are watching over us and are proud of what we have become. Thank you, Jehovah, for peace in the chaos and stillness so I can rest. Please keep Carli safe.
In Jesus' name, we pray. Amen.
Mirabel

Chapter 17: Surprise

TIFFANY

I did it. I finished a year of intense coursework learning the holistic side of skincare. Those classes did so much more for me in a short time than any other school I'd gone to, and let me tell you there have been a lot. There was interior design, business management, dental hygiene, nursing, and now skincare. I liked to have my hand in as many pots as possible.

I was inspired to fuel my talents as much as possible in this life. The common denominator: I wanted to help others. I wanted to help them in a deeper way. I wanted to help heal their lives in ways they ever thought possible, which is why holistic health was my passion. Going through this program, I learned so much about healing at deeper levels. Hell, this entire program has been therapy for me. I was nervous about embarking on an entirely new journey, but I was excited. Moving to Florida to further my studies was going to be so great for me. The love of my life already there and waiting was the icing on the cake.

It was hard to relish in the excitement of my life because Carli's antics took precedence over everything in the family. My aunt Yolanda and I spoke daily about Carli. No one could understand what she was doing or even why. We just knew she needed to get home and get herself together ASAP.

My mom didn't seem stressed out about Carli. Honestly, she knew Carli so well that she was confident she'd make her return. My mom was adamant about us just leaving Carli alone.

Brianna and I checked in daily. Her sisters were disgusted with her. I also reassured them that Carli would be back if given time.

Eventually, I told my Aunt Yolanda that I no longer wanted to hear about the crazy behavior Carli exhibited on Twitter.

My mom planned a nice quiet dinner for my graduation. I had a wine night with the girls last night, and I was still feeling every bit of it. Since we were going for BBQ, I threw on a sundress and went to eat!

I was happy to celebrate this accomplishment despite being discouraged along the way. My parents and family supported my move and were excited to see me spread my wings. Upon graduating, I prayed, which I do every morning on the way to class and work. On the morning of my last day of class, I prayed that God protects me on this new journey. I asked him to reveal and remove any negative people or things that would not serve me on this journey. I prayed for the strength of my family to be okay without me as I moved. I also prayed for peace and wisdom over any challenges I would face in this new and scary time of my life.

We arrived that evening to the dinner, and to my surprise, my mom invited everyone that supported me over this year. I looked down the table and saw my aunts and uncles on my dad's side, Aunt Pearl and my cousins. WOW, they grew up! The twins sat down at the end and other family and close friends. And my girls, my two best friends, were there too! Brianna saved me a seat and urged me to try the beer she ordered. She offered to get me the same.

She did it again! My mom surprised me with everyone I loved, and we enjoyed a fantastic BBQ dinner. My heart was full.

Of course, the topic of Carli came up, and we all sounded off on how we felt about her behavior.

"I can't believe her. I am so done with her ass. She is so disrespectful. After everything your mom and dad have done for all of us. They built her ass a room and everything," Brianna said, piercing the last few fries on her plate.

"It's just unfortunate. I'm just so disappointed in Carli right now. Our mom would be so upset with her. Like, we didn't even get to go to graduation. Like, after all that, and she acts like this." Alana, the more emotional one, said while fighting back tears.

Brianna stroked the shoulder of her twin. Then she turned to me and said they loved us and apologized for everything. I told her not to be sorry. We're family. We go through shit, but then we forgive, and we move on.

"Has she reached out or anything? We know she's been on Twitter, according to Aunt Yolanda." Said my mom to Alana.

The twins in unison, "Yep!"

"The last time she called asking for money was maybe two weeks ago. I told her not ever call me again asking for money. That the next time she calls me, she better have *a reason* to call me!" Alana giving her final argument on the matter, and the conversation moved on.

Brianna, piggybacking off of her sister's tone. "She needs to apologize to you guys."

"I told you guys over and over again, we do not need an apology. We're parents. We know how this goes. We just want the girl safe." My mom, the voice of reason chimed in.

"I know, right! I still want to kill her!" Brianna laughed.

We all laughed aloud, laughter was our thing.

We took and posted a beautiful group photo where we all looked so happy and beaming. I cherish that day because I knew this would be one of the last times we could all get together before my move. It was also a day that we all needed after the Carli chaos of the previous month. We deserved a moment to laugh, to eat, and to be a celebratory family, not one always in struggle.

We'd hoped Carli would see our posts and come home. We'd had high hopes that for a quick second, she would remember the love we all shared. That she knew we would accept her despite her behavior. I probably couldn't say the same for her sisters, but I knew my parents maintained they just wanted her safe and taking care of herself. Based on her Twitter posts, that didn't seem like the case.

I was pissed at her, but in all honesty, I was worried about her. I was unsure why Alana said she'd needed some huge reason to come home. I know she royally fucked up, but I'd hoped that if she were in trouble, any one of our doors would be open. The family I knew us to be, we always pull together in struggle. We were the strongest women I knew. Strength was becoming our thing.

Chapter 18: The Longest Wednesday Ever

MIRABEL

Farrell was set to go on his biennial business trip to Atlanta, Georgia. He was so excited about this trip as he would be attending some new workshops and receiving an award. I was so proud of him. Through all of my family's drama, he remained true to taking care of his family, me, and what we have. I was unable to join him on this trip because of my daycare. Other families rely on me, so I rarely take time off. He knew I was with him in spirit.

Tiffany came to drop him off at the airport. I am thankful for a child old enough to help out as she does, no questions asked. A honk came from the driveway, and I kissed my husband, wished him good luck, and told him I loved him dearly. "I love you too, honey!" he said as he got into Tiffany's car and headed down the driveway.

The day continued on as normal. Tiffany returned home from work later that evening. We decided to skip out on our weekly workout together. I had a slight headache and just wanted to relax tonight. I retreated up to my room after the last of my children left. A hot shower and cup of chamomile tea were awaiting me. When my husband was away on business, I loved sitting in his recliner with my tea while watching Wendy Williams, The Real, or his least favorite, Lifetime Movie Network. This was my downtime that I adored so much.

Just as I began steeping my tea before getting into the shower, my cell rang. It was Alana.

"Hey, Mirabel. It's Alana," she said in her most cheerful voice.

"Hey, Alana, what's up?!"

"I have Carli here and—um—she wants to apologize to you guys. I told her she has to apologize to you."

"Alana," slightly confused, I continued. "I keep telling you guys Carli does not have to apologize to us. She's eighteen. She's going through something right now. I am just glad she is with you. Let's just let it be that and move on."

"Okay—um—well, Carli is saying some other things. She's right here."

"What?"

"Mirabel, please just let us come up there."

"Alana, what is Carli saying?"

"Please just let us come up there."

"Alana, what is Carli saying?"

"Well, where's Farrell?"

"He's in Atlanta. He won't be back until Monday."

"Okay. Hmmm."

"You don't have to come all the way up here. What is Carli saying?" My heart pounded incredulously. What is she about to tell me?

"Carli is saying that Farrell was molesting her."

"WHAT!" Deep breath in. "Okay." Deep breath out. "Okay, Alana. I have to go. I'll call you back."

My life flashed before my eyes. I wasn't sure how I made it down the stairs in one piece, but I made it. My knees eventually buckled before my daughter.

"Carli is saying Farrell has been molesting her." Tears streamed down my face. All the hurt over the last five years, which I tried to stuff down, came to surface. It wasn't until the reflection on my daughter's face at this moment that I knew that I was broken.

"SHE'S FUCKING LYING!" Tiffany grabbed her phone and began texting Brianna. "YOUR FUCKING SISTER IS A—"

Delete.

She slipped her sandals on, grabbed her purse, and ran toward the door. My son was upstairs, unknowing of what just happened. I pulled to Tiffany. "Tiffany! Where are you going?"

"To beat her ass! I can't believe her. Oh, so this is her reason to come back? Are you fucking kidding me?"

"Tiffany no. We don't know where she's going with this. We need to be smart!"

Tiffany stepped outside to phone Brianna, her confidant, to figure this out.

"Hey, cousin," Brianna answered.

"Hi. How are you guys? Where is she?" Tiffany asked.

"She's in the house with Alana. I came to my car to talk. She's fine. We're just trying to comfort her."

"Okay. I'm glad she's okay. So what exactly happened?"

"I was at work. She texts Alana saying she had something to tell her. The next text said, 'Farrell was molesting me.' Alana said she went crazy at work and started throwing up. Alana texts me. I freaked out and left work and went to pick her up. It was weird because she was right down the street at her friend's house. She said she told her friend's mom. I'm not sure. I didn't ask because Carli had me pick her up on the corner. Anyways I picked her up and brought her home and let her sleep. When Alana got home, we talked to her more. When we got her home, we sat her down and asked her questions. She answered. She said he would come down at eleven o'clock pm each night, no penetration. He would always lay on top of the covers and rub her body up and down and call her sexy. I asked if she ever saw him naked, she said no."

"Okay, when did this start?"

"She said it started when she was fifteen. When she got her room."

"Brianna, do you believe her, honestly?

"Honestly? No, I didn't believe it at first because we know Farrell. Like, yea right. But then she was balling crying acting all crazy, so I had to—"

"The same theatrics she does when she has to do the dishes? This is a very sensitive situation, Brianna. I know it needs to be taken seriously but look at the facts. Number one: I know this didn't happen because I live here and am up all times of the night. Two: you guys said she needed a reason to contact you, and just after she sees us all together happy and smiling, she pulls this! I've been around this man since I was two years old. This is not in his character, and you know it!"

"I know it's crazy. Her track record is not good with all the lying she's been doing. We told her that. She fully understands how serious this is to just be saying it, ya know. I mean, it happens, and this is not something to play about. I know people it's happened to."

"Oh, I know it does. It just didn't happen in my house. I know that for a fact, but I'll keep the reasons why until we can meet as a family and talk about this."

"I know this is so crazy. We love Farrell. I hope it's not true. Just ask him, Tiffany. Just look into his eyes, and you'll know."

"You do the same. I don't believe her. I understand where you stand. You have to ride for yours, and I have to ride for mine. We'll see how this plays out."

They got off the phone. My sister Tammy arrived, and we all sat dejected, rejected, and objecting to the very idea that this was the reality we were facing. Farrell hadn't made it to Atlanta before all of this went down. He has no idea the suffering that was taking place back home.

We sat in silence while waiting for Farrell to answer the S.O.S. Tammy sat starring off into the future; she said she saw an orange jumpsuit. Murder was painted on her lips that stayed pursed to prevent the evil that would slip out. Tiffany stared at the ground, focused. Drew sat on the counter of the kitchen, scared. We tried to keep it from him as long as possible, but the kid was smart. He broke down. His father might be facing jail time over a lie, our family broken, our spirits crying out for help and no one to reach for. My rock was thousands of miles away, and I was having a hard time being strong for those looking to me for strength.

No one said a word until my daughter, ever so bold, broke the growing silence. Her words straight to my heart. "YOU DON'T BELIEVE IT? DO YOU?"

Taking a deep breath in, answering from my soul, I let out a tired, "No. I don't know why Carli is doing this."

Drew whispered through his broken, pubescent vocals, "Why would she *do* this to us?"

"I don't know, son. I don't know."

"She did this to get back in good graces with her sisters. That's why." Tiffany is now directing her anger to the elephant in the room.

"We don't know where she is going with this, so tread lightly talking to them," I told my children, who I raised to love and respect family. What just happened here?

My phone rang. It was my husband. His phone had died, and the frustration, angst, and fear grew to unbearable heights.

"Honey!"

"Hey, honey. What's up?!"

"HONEY!" A bit more anxiety came through the phone and shot straight to *his* heart.

"Honey, what's going on?"

"Carli told Alana and Brianna that you were molesting her."

An echo came through the phone as the love of my life shouted in the same fear I knew we couldn't save each other from.

"WHAT!! OH NO. NO. NO. NO. THIS ISNT HAPPENING. NO. NO."

The sound of desperation sliced the air as his cries filled the spaces in between my own whimpers. We sat and cried together.

"Honey, why is she doing this? Why is she doing this?"

"I don't know, Tiffany has been talking to Brianna."

"What should I do? Should I catch a flight back? What do we do to prove my innocence? I want to talk to my kids."

"No, honey, just do what you need to do there. You'll be back in a couple days. We'll go from there. I'll tell Tiffany to call when we're done talking."

"Honey, I *did not* do this. Please believe me. I can't believe this is happening."

"We just need to pray, honey. Pray."

TIFFANY

Maybe I was a bit insensitive. My truth was that I was not, I reacted. Hearing the accusation towards the man I'd been around since I was two years old was bizarre. Especially knowing the dynamics that we've established in the home. The bond I'd seen her develop as being the oldest in the home under eighteen. She was extremely happy here. None of that seems to matter right now. My phone rang. It was my dad.

"Hey, baby girl." No matter how old we got, my sister and I were always his baby girls. I know even saying hello was difficult for him. We all needed each other right now as we couldn't be together. Nonetheless, the roller coaster was just beginning.

"Hi, are you okay?"

"No." whimpering off.

I've seen my father dance. I've heard him spit the best rhymes ever. I've seen him speak at large business events. That cold Wednesday night was the first time I heard my father cry.

I couldn't hold back my pains either. Crying yet getting down to business was the Capricorn way; he knew I was going to approach.

"I don't know why she is doing this. I am just going to ask, did you do any of this?"

"No, I did not. I give you my word as a man. The man you know me to be. I did not do this."

"Okay. Then we ride this wave 'til it's over. I don't believe it. I'm maintaining that until the end."

"I Love you, baby girl."

"I love you too, Pops."

Dear Jehovah,

I come to you with an open heart that weeps. A heart that was shattered today at the whisper of such chilling words that will forever change the dynamic of my family structure.

The accusations brought on to the man who took care of me the last twenty-six years. The man who stepped in and stepped up where another man lacked majorly. These accusations—these words of hate spoken on his name will forever be heard in the ears of all of us. Carli's lies and deceit and utter disrespect finally did what she always intended to do—break this family at its core.

Jehovah, I wish I could turn back time when things were good. Just eight hours ago, life was simple. Life was complete. Life was joyous. Tonight I pray from a place of pain. I pray that these accusations come to light as false and entirely made up as a means of attention-grabbing.

I pray that we, as a family, can forgive her for her mentally unstable ways and move forward. Today I was disgusted with humanity. I was ill at the thought of family. It hurt to hear my dad cry and apologize for the untruth that Carli spoke. I watched my mom go weak in the knees. I watched my usually outspoken aunt go silent—plagued with anger. I watched my little brother, a kid who adores his father, cry at the thought of losing him, of losing our family. I watched myself crumble piece by piece, not recognizing this life anymore.

I pray that we can wake up in the morning with a fresh start and decide how to handle this to protect and prove his innocence. Every cell, bone, and muscle fiber in my body knows not only is he incapable of such actions. I know in my heart that he would NEVER cross that line or even think about it. He's seen me grow from a two-year-old in diapers to a twenty-eight-year-old woman and has never made me feel uncomfortable in any way. This is the man who knocks on any door a woman may be behind. The man who waits for the say-so before entering. This man respects the privacy of women and respects the boundaries of women, even in his own home. I'm torn at my core, Jehovah, because, for once, none of us know where to turn. My mom is lost without my dad, her rock here. I am lost because I see her, my rock in front of me crumbling at the thought of what is to come. Sadly, I see my brother scared for his future.

I rebuke the devil in the name of Jesus to back away from this house. I pray that God restores what is right and well in our home and restores the strength of this family. I ask that you place your hands on our heavy hearts and protect us for the days to come. Help us be triumphant in your name as we embark on this journey ahead. I pray For Carli to reveal the truth and for her to get the help she needs at this scary time in her life.

In Jesus' name, we pray. Amen.

Tiffany

FARRELL

Here I was in Atlanta on a trip that was supposed to be rewarding for my career. I'd just arrive in my hotel room when the news of Carli's accusations sent my world spinning. A million thoughts went through my head. How do I prove this is a lie? How do I show I'm innocent? How do I do that? It was going to be my word against hers. The authorities always believe the woman. My stomach curdled. Sweat beads formed at the base of my neck. Damn.

Was I facing jail time? What about our businesses? Licensing? What about my wife's daycare?

My wife. I had to make sure she knew this was not the truth, let me start there, first things first.

First of all, this is untrue. This has never happened, and I have no idea as to what prompted this girl even to say this.

My stomach was in knots, and I could barely talk. I felt like crying. I was afraid, sad, hurt, and mostly I'm confused. Was this a dream? A nightmare? WAKE UP, FARELL! WAKE UP!

Given the expense, we agreed that I'd finish the Atlanta trip. I did my best to be present and do what I came to do. When I get home, we'd get on top of the Carli issue and handle it as a family. First, I needed to comfort my wife and make sure she understood that I was innocent—that this was a lie in every way, shape, and form.

On to the legality of this. I knew my innocence, but I had assets to protect and needed to consult legal counsel in the event that I was handcuffed upon my return. I had to be prepared and move cautiously. Who do I even ask about such a matter?

Later that evening, my wife told me that my daughter Tiffany had been in contact with the twins. They agreed to have a family meeting as soon as I returned. Great! Let's do it! I was ready to clear my name and let them know I would never do such a thing.

MIRABEL

What had my life become? I really had no time to deal with the emotional side of this. This was a very crazy situation for all of us. Right now, the twins were adamant about keeping communication and the situation between us until we could all meet to discuss. We agreed to do so the day Farrell got back in town.

They each keep texting me. They asked if I was okay and if we needed anything. It's evident, at this point, they believe their sister. I'm okay with that. However, nowhere in my spirit did I believe this happened in my home.

Number one: I'm nosey. My husband is not crazy. I would never tolerate anything like this. Two: This was the man I brought around my daughter. Let's face it, I would never have a man around my own daughter that I even thought was capable of something this disgusting. If I suspected, yes, he would be gone. Period. I don't play about this kind of stuff. I am anxious to meet with everyone so we can talk about this. This was their request, and we are happy to oblige.

My chamomile tea was now ice cold. The tea bag settled to the bottom of my mug, something like my heart in the pit of my stomach. I restarted my shower and stood there numb to the heat penetrating my skin. I prayed, but mostly I cried. I washed off what would become the longest Wednesday ever.

Dear Jehovah,
I need your strength.
In Jesus' name, we pray. Amen.
Mirabel

Chapter 19: The Morning After

TIFFANY

Last night was a blur. I spent most of the evening pacing up and down the driveway of our home. I remembered the good times: The parked cars lined up valet style for the countless family gatherings, and laughter floating through the night air that was once so consoling. Today our home on the hill seemed so dark, dismal, and lonely.

I talked to the man who raised me last night. I needed to hear him say the words. Hell, I needed to know I had the courage just to ask him. I knew he did not do this, but I knew how serious this was. I had to act accordingly. My desire to go whoop Carli's ass was still present. However, for now, we needed to go into protect mode and unify to prove his innocence.

The very next day after Carli let the lie escape her lips, our lives changed. My mother reluctantly opened her daycare to care for kids, not hers, when she could do little to nothing to comfort her own. Her husband, our father, was gone, and we had nowhere to turn.

I went to work and did my best to hide the troubles at home. I tried to put my troubles behind me despite not knowing whether I'd need to help out at home should an arrest be made. We went into protect mode while the twins and Carli continued on with regular programming.

I spent the day gathering texts between Aunt Yolanda and me and between Brianna and me as evidence of Carli's mental space just one month ago. These conversations also highlighted how they felt about Carli and her character leading up to the events. Pertinent information that we might need later. I created a file and started saving item after item for later use. My years of *Law and Order SVU* were finally beginning to pay off.

While preparing my data, I continued to get texts and calls from Brianna. Since her mom passed, I've always been her source of comfort, genuine love, and just plain logic. I was the big cousin I was supposed to be.

This time I had nothing to offer. I was too afraid to ask for what I needed from her. I wanted her to take a step back and look at the bigger picture and believe what she knew to be true about my dad. I didn't have the courage, not because I was afraid, but I knew I couldn't flat out accuse Carli of lying. I was in disbelief because in today's society, if a woman says it happened, it happened. At least that's what they'll think.

"Hi, cousin. How are you? I'm going crazy. I couldn't sleep last night!"

"Eh, I'm okay. How is Carli?"

"She's fine. She's at the community college doing a cheer thing she begged us to go to. I came to the races with friends. I need a drink or ten after yesterday. Ha-ha!"

"You're where?"

"The races. My friend invited me, so I came to destress. Yesterday was too much!"

"I see. Well, have fun. I am at work. I'll talk to you later."

"Okay. Wait. Did your mom tell you we are all meeting when Farrell gets back next Monday?"

"Yes, she did."

"Okay, yay! Love you, cousin!" Brianna playfully exited one of the last conversations we would have.

I couldn't muster up the words to say 'I love you too'. Right now, I couldn't decide what I felt about family, love, or loyalty. All I knew was this was probably the worst pain I'd ever felt. The people that I'd grown so accustomed to giving and receiving comfort from were standing on the front lines ready to shoot. This time the target was on our backs.

Helpless was a better word to describe the collective feeling of this family. Helpless. Who do we turn to when we've been the source of everyone's comfort, the hub of love for a family whose main theme has been distress? Who do you run to when the woes of the world get too heavy? We had nowhere to turn but up. I somehow had to remain strong for my mom. I had to continue to reassure her that Carli had no grounds or evidence to back her story. I had to be strong for my baby brother, who just so desperately needed a hug from his best friend, our dad.

We made a pact to limit as much conversation with them up until the meeting. This also meant limited contact for Drew. Carli might attempt to reach him, which for Drew would be hard because they were very close. We had to make him understand how serious this was. After all, he was the only child being affected by these lies.

The meeting was set for next Wednesday. Me, Mom, Pops, Drew, Aunt Tammy, the twins, and Carli. We had full confidence that when we all met, this would be hashed out. I promised my mother I would keep my hands to myself.

FARRELL

The worst thing happened to me as a man. I didn't know what to do, where to turn, or who to tell. How the hell was I going to prove I would never? These were the thoughts that plagued the first day of my long-awaited business trip. A trip that only happens every few years. A trip that we saved up for a year for me to go on. I was super excited to be attending workshops and participating this year. Being present for my team in this way was a goal I've had set for a while, but here it was unfolding in the ugliest way possible.

An infomercial buzzed on the TV, but I sat in my hotel room deaf to the sounds around me. I was numb to my own breath. I had to do my best to be as present as while here. Lord knows all I wanted was to be home with my family.

Lord. That's where we have to put our strength. The Lord was the only one who could fix this. I had faith that he would soothe my sorrows as I fought for my innocence. Damn it, I would fight.

MIRABEL

I couldn't stop crying. My heart ached in a way that could not be measured. I was lost and afraid to say so. I needed my mother. I needed someone to tell me what the fuck to do. How do I make them understand that this was serious, that I was not ignoring them or her, but I knew for a fact this did not happen? If I was wrong, I would help them lock him up and move on. Let me just put it out there, so no one thought I was delusional. I knew I was not wrong. I knew Carli was happy here. They knew Carli was happy here. Everyone knew Carli was happy here, so why were we being tested?

I needed someone to lean on. Someone with logic and common sense. Someone that I respected highly—that my own mother highly respected. I called my Aunt Francis, the more level headed of my mother's siblings. She didn't get caught up in the family drama. I called her, and she became the shoulder I so desperately needed. She was the matriarch on the west coast, and I needed her guidance.

My Aunt always knew what to say. I told her what happened. The anger that exuded from that phone was oddly reassuring that *someone* was on our side—*someone* believed our truth. The "Oh boy" she let out after I revealed my ugly reality noted how bad this was. When she remarked how twisted Cara and her girls were, I was shocked to hear her speak of her own deceased sister that way. We all know Cara had an evil side. I just didn't expect to hear about it right *now*.

Francis let me know she'd be here if I needed her. She told me she believed us and knew Carli was trouble. She was sorry we are going through this. She reassured me that she would come to town on my behalf, and she would be there if we needed it. I need all the support I could get.

Tiffany was reluctant for me to call, but I'm glad I did. I felt understood and safe. This would have to do until my husband returned home in a few days.

Right now, at this very moment, I didn't have a fighting bone in my body. I had to let the emotions out first and armor myself with the word of God to be able to move through this. Jehovah, my God, was my connection to my mother and grandmother. I would ask him for the strength to weather the storm that I created by bringing her into my home. I had to forgive myself. I hoped my family did too. My intentions were good. They are still good and will continue to be good as we fight the fight of our family, the fight for my marriage, and, hell, the fight of my life.

Dear Jehovah
I just need the strength, just for today, to proceed the way you will have us to go. Please protect my family, my husband, my home, and businesses. Soothe my aching heart. That's all I can muster up for today, Jehovah.
In Jesus' name, we pray. Amen.
Mirabel

Chapter 20: Family Meeting

MIRABEL

Farrell was returning tonight. I was ready for this to be done and over with. I was prepared to meet this head-on.

Tiffany seemed to believe it was going to blow over, and Carli would need some sort of mental help after. While I didn't deny the need for help, I also believed that my child didn't get that this could become ugly before it got better. That's why we were adamant about the meeting.

The days marched along slowly. Our phones continuously lit up with texts and calls from the twins trying to get Carli situated and established into adulthood. So far, Brianna called four times asking about birth certificates and paperwork to get Carli enrolled in school. I obliged and sent them whatever I had. I was in no way interested in hindering her progression in life, even if she was trying to take mine away.

My phone rang for a fifth time. This time it was Alana.

"Hey, Mirabel. It's Alana. Do you have a minute?"

Always so professional, that Alana, "Yes. What's going on?"

"When is Farrell getting home because we need to handle this?"

"Alana, I already told you he gets in tonight. We agreed to meet this week as a family. If that doesn't work for you, then we can come when I pick him up from the airport, not a problem. No one is running."

"We'll we will wait for *you*, but we aren't doing *shit* for Farrell. And actually, we were talking to Carli, and she doesn't want to meet with the family anyways."

"Okay, what does that mean? We have to talk about this, Alana."

"We think it would be best if you and Tiffany just came. She doesn't want to face Farrell right now."

"She had no problem with him up until she said this crap, but okay, fine, we can meet Wednesday around seven. I'll let Tiffany know."

"Okay, she's just been throwing up, crying, and freaking out every time we mention the meeting." Sure she is.

"Okay, Alana. No problem we will be there Wednesday at seven."

"Okay. Love you!"

"Love you too."

Alana has a way of coming off pushy and quite annoying, but I knew better than to feed into any of this. I had a home to protect. I told Tiffany that she and I were going down there to meet with them. We'd try to hash as much of this out as possible.

That Wednesday evening, when Tiffany got home from work, we packed up her car with Carli's remaining items; a few boxes, a few bags of clothes, and some trash. We decided to take her things and make this clean break while we figured this out. Tiffany was dying to sage the house but wouldn't until all remnants of her were gone.

Together, my daughter and I drove down to the twin's home. There we would find Carli dressed in a beautiful pink sundress, eyes normal and bright, not a tear in sight. A cat paced the floor, and smells of lavender filled their small space. The three of them sat on the sectional couch. A chair was placed in the middle of the floor, facing the couch. The hot seat in the middle, I presumed, was for me. We entered the home, my heart racing, anxiety rising but keeping me grounded at the same time. I came here to clear our name.

"Thank you for having us here to talk. I don't even know what happened here. How do we go from getting ready for graduation, planning a dinner, and planning a move to this?"

"Mirabel, stop—"

"No, see you invited *me* here, so I am going to talk first. You guys have been the ones doing *all* the talking, so it's time you listen."

All three pairs of eyes froze in unison.

"We are talking about a man who has taken care of my mother, my grandmother, your grandmother, and your mother. This is the man who has been there when no one else was. He was there when your father shot your mother. So, before we get into the details, I want you to think about what *you* know Farrell to be to *each* of you."

Alana chimed in the annoying way she does. "Look, Mirabel, you're not going to come in my house talking shit like that. We can just call the cops and be done with it. You don't come in here and—"

Brianna, now growing louder over her sister, "BUT THE CHILD SAID IT HAPPENED. WE HAVE TO BELIEVE HER!"

"Look, ladies, the energy here is growing negative. This is a touchy subject. We need to remember to come from a place of love, everyone chill! Agreed?" Tiffany leveled the energy of the meeting, and we proceeded.

Still calm and ready to hear whatever was coming my way, I handled myself well in their DIY hot seat.

"You're saying all of this about character and all that which I get. Carli is saying it happened, so this is a hard place for us too because we loved Farrell, but this can be proven Carli wrote a poem about it."

"A Poem?"

"Yes, it had the date stamp for February. I saw it. And I don't like how you're not even trying to hear us out. This was supposed to be a meeting."

"You're right, I haven't spoken to the person I need to speak to, the reason why we're all here."

Turning to Carli nestled in the corner of the couch, disconnected from the current reality she created.

"Carli, do you have something you need to tell me?"

Whispering softly, "No."

"I'm sorry, Carli. Speak up. Do you have something you want to say?"

"No, you can finish."

The twins glanced from Carli back to me and continued to defend their baby sister.

"This is the man that Carli would call to kill spiders in her room." Brianna shot a look to Carli in almost disgust.

Tiffany looked to Carli. "Carli, *if* this did happen, why are you *just* saying something now?"

As meek, as she could, she whispered, "I didn't want to break up the family or break up the *perfect couple.*" Her eyes shuffled to find their focus in her hands as she quietly and inadvertently revealed her initial intention.

"We have done everything we can for Carli, I don't under—"

"Mirabel, we get all that you have done, and we're not talking about you. This is about Farrell. You're lucky we are even talking. We could have had the cops show up and arrest his ass!"

"As far as I'm concerned, we are one," I said as a matter of fact.

"This is the same man who I watched grow helpless when he couldn't help his own daughter Iman through her struggles. A man that Carli highly respected and was comfortable around just like you guys have always been. I don't know where this is going to go. I am highly disappointed in this family. Grandma would be so upset. I understand y'all have to do what you have to do so we'll just go from there, I guess. So, um, we have the rest of Carli's items in the car if you guys want to come unload."

And like that, I made my case and made my way to the door. The three of them shuffled to put shoes on to come down to the car to bring her items in. I sat in the front seat of my daughter's car and exhaled to prevent the downpour of tears. While they unloaded the car, I stayed about-face, to prepare myself for the war ahead.

Dear Jehovah,

My family dynamics are changing, and only you know the reason. I pray that you cover my family in your grace and strengthen us as we proceed. I don't know where to go right now, God. I could use my mother's advice right now. I feel helpless and lost. I pray you offer peace just for my home tonight so we can face the fight ahead. I pray you cover my husband and protect his freedom. I pray you change Carli's heart and help us to come together as a family. I know your will, will be had on this situation. I trust you and this process.

In Jesus' name, we pray. Amen.

Mirabel

TIFFANY

The meeting went exactly how I expected. It was as peaceful as it could be. I kept my hands to myself, but I was ready if hands needed tossing. I sat there as a mediator, mostly. Carli sat to the right of me. The twins to her right. My mother sat in the seat in the middle of the floor. As if this was supposed to intimidate her. Ha.

She sat and delivered a clear and direct message, all without getting loud or crazy. I have so much to learn from her because I don't know how she did it.

Carli sat disconnected in the corner, watching the stringed-dance of the puppet show she created. She spoke the words and was now having her sisters fight her battle. Typical. When my mom gave her the floor to speak, she said nothing. This was the time I was preparing myself to hear her speak lies on my father, but she said nothing. We were all a little shocked, but it was short-lived as the twins continued to plead her case.

Once we were finished, my mom left her hot seat and made her way out the door. I followed suit to make this goodbye as painless as possible.

I slipped my shoes onto my feet and handed Brianna an old bag of clothes I had borrowed a few months ago. I figured I should return them before things get awkward because, after today, I fully expected them too. She looked in the bag and laughed as she tied it back up. I reached in for a hug, and we met in the middle. I held her a bit longer that day. I nestled her into me as we hugged, letting her know that I loved her so much. I had to ride with the truth even if that meant riding alone. Somehow I knew this would be the last time I would see my baby cousin, the last time I would feel close to her like a sister. I hugged her one last time to take in all her warmth, softness, laughter, and comfort. After all, my cousins were my first friends. We were true blue and tight like glue. *This* should be a moment we come together. Cousins should be able to lean on each other when the rest of the family was going crazy. The cousin relationship is the one that is supposed to go untouched. It is no coincidence that at that moment, we filled each other up only to release each other without even knowing it.

Chapter 21: The Aftermath

MIRABEL

I didn't recognize my life anymore. There was a darkness that crept through the halls and into my spirit that I couldn't shake. I looked around my home and remembered the vibrancy it held when it was filled with those that I loved the most. I tried so hard not to break down. I got up daily to care for these beautiful children who needed me. I was worried about this affecting my business. I didn't have a clue as to where they were going to take this, seeing that Carli had nothing to say about *anything* when met. I had to be prepared either way. Having your own business had always been our goal, and here I was, kicking myself for not staying in the corporate setting. At least then I wouldn't be at risk of losing my income, my home, or my mind.

I worked with children and was damn good at it if I must say. This was my calling and my purpose. At that moment of losing it all, I recognize how much I loved what I did. To think, all I was trying to was prevent our baby cousin from the vicious cycle of the system.

Having Farrell home was calming to my mind. Just having him to cry to, vent to, and pick this apart allowed us to see the raw emotions of fear, disappointment, and anger. We've always been close, but for some reason, this has brought us closer spiritually. We decided to arm ourselves with the word of God. That was all I could count on right now because man had been a complete fail.

We knelt nightly to protect each other. He reassured me that he would never do such a thing. We talked about her time here in the home, how content she was, and how much she loved the family unit. Now *my* family was under attack. We wanted to crumble but couldn't because there is no one to catch us.

My local relatives were in town this weekend. I decided to close my daycare just to enjoy a three-day weekend with what little family we had left. This was my Aunt on my deceased fathers' side. She was a part of the New York clan who stepped up to be there for us during this insanely difficult time. They came down to visit with their grandkids for the weekend, and they were staying at our place. It felt good to have my home filled again with kind spirits and laughter.

Unfortunately, fear was the elephant in the room we couldn't ignore. No matter the distraction, my mind automatically drifted back to what happened. I couldn't seem to grasp that this was my reality. Damn it, I was fighting for my fucking family like a mama bear. Just as I started to feel my strength rising, a faint knock was heard at the daycare's front door.

Farrell walked downstairs and answered the door.

"Hi, is Mirabel Davis available?"

"Yes, may I tell her who is here?"

"Robert Moore, Daycare Licensing Investigative Unit."

"Ok. What is this regarding?"

"The welfare of a child. Can we please speak to Mirabel?"

Farrell closed the door softly and marched up the stairs and pulled me aside. He quickly and quietly explained to me what was going on. In an effort not to alarm anyone, I went outside and spoke to them. I let them know that I was, in fact, closed for the day that any further investigating would have to be done once I am open.

The two investigators were friendly, considering the news they had to deliver. They were shocked that I'd been in business for nearly fifteen years and never had a blemish on my license or an issue with a child.

I never had a complaint. I always received rave reviews from pop up licensing visits and rave reviews with childcare programs in my community. I partnered with a preschool near our home when they had an overflow. Their kids got the best level of care with me. I was at a loss for words but didn't have time to wallow. It was time to get busy gathering our evidence to build our case. This complaint was the beginning of the process we so dreaded but knew would come. We were ready. We were unified. Here we go.

The following week, we watched the driveway intently. Halfway expecting a police car to show up and halfway expecting an apologetic Carli to come running home. Fortunately, and unfortunately enough, neither happened. The anxiety in each of us grew.

Round one of investigative hell, began that following Thursday. Two women entered my home, called the shots, disrespected my husband, belittled me, and I could do nothing about it. One was from the state and one a caseworker representing the local licensing department. This experience was far different from the visit from one week ago. These women pushed into my home, counted children, asked for records for each of them, and reviewed meal plans. They were doing the norm of what a routine licensing visit would be with a bitchy undertone and control included. I had to remember they were here to do a job. I had to comply with honesty and grace like my life depended on it, well, because it did at this point.

The two women set up shop upstairs with their laptops and pads of paper ready to drill. I went up first while Tiffany and Farrell sat downstairs with the children who were just put down for their nap time.

We sat upstairs in my living room, although at this moment, none of this seems real. My space was virtually unrecognizable. I did my best to sit as poised as possible. The anxiety crept up the small of my back and settled in the pit of my stomach. I took a deep breath and mustered the courage to answer the many questions they had.

"Ma'am, please state your name for the record."

She clicked her small silver tape recorder on. The flashing light hypnotized me as I opened my mouth to plead the case of my life.

"Mirabel Davis."

"Thank you, we can proceed. Mirabel, there has been a claim filed for child abuse. Are you aware of this claim?'

"My cousin?" I asked abruptly.

The two women looked at each other. The one from the state jotted down a few notes as they proceeded.

"Why would you ask that specifically?"

"My cousin called me and told me my other cousin, Carli, made these accusations a week ago."

More jotting.

I proceeded as they urged me to be as thorough as possible. Again not fully understanding what just happened, I gave the two women the facts from the beginning.

"I cared for my cousin for five years after my aunt died. She just turned eighteen a month ago. She called on her last day of school, asking if she can walk to the Mexican restaurant by her school to get a burrito. I told her I didn't care. Hours later, my husband nor I heard anything from her, so we started calling. Finally, she returned my call and said she went to the mall, stating that I said, 'I didn't care.' She then tells my husband I make her uncomfortable and that she would be coming to the home to get her items that were already packed. When she got here, she handed me her graduation tickets. I gave them back, letting her know that I wouldn't be going since she expressed that I make her uncomfortable. I didn't want to ruin her special day. She got her items and left. A few weeks later, we go to dinner to celebrate my daughter's move and graduation with the family. Two days after that, I get a call from Alana, her sister, saying Carli made these accusations that my husband did this, and here we are."

The women from licensing who sat unconvinced asked passively, "Do you believe it."

"ABSOLUTELY NOT."

The same woman peering down from behind her glasses that sat on the edge of her nose. "If it was true, then what?"

No longer fighting back the tears or the shiver that came up my spine. "Then, I lose everything. My world is upside down."

"Did you allow this in your home, Mrs. Davis?"

"With all due respect, there was nothing to allow because it didn't happen."

"You said you have text conversations with her and her sisters, correct?"

"Yes, I do." I reached for my phone and allowed them to read the text thread from Carli and me on her last day of school. I allowed them to read text messages from Brianna and Alana regarding Carli from the last month. I allowed them to read text threads between me and my husband, my daughter, and Yolanda. I didn't care. Read it all.

I was exposed, raw, real, and ready to fight for my truth. I know this happens, trust me having a daughter I am vastly aware that this happens. Hell, it's actually happened in our family with other members whom I've kept my kids away from. No doubt, I know this happens. It just didn't happen in my home.

After reading through countless messages, they informed me that there was an active investigation. They asked for any additional and pertinent information as well as any other family members to contact. I gave them Yolanda's information since she was in contact with Carli during that month she disappeared. Maybe she'll have some insight into this. The investigation should be easy as long as she told the truth about her own experiences in my home and with Carli the last few months.

I couldn't believe I was under investigation. My business was being investigated because I worked with children. My home was being investigated because I worked from home. I was being investigated because I had too big of a heart. I could literally lose everything—my home, family, business, livelihood, and the love of my life.

Speaking of him, they asked to see him next. I proceeded down the stairs and into the daycare and summoned him to the hot seat.

FARELL

Seeing defeat replace strength on my wife's face, I knew what was coming next was not going to be pleasant. My daughter and I sat in the daycare, praying that this investigation went well. That my truth would be heard. My life depended on it. I hugged my wife and pushed what little strength I had left into her as I proceeded up the dark stairway. With each step, I tried to brace myself for the unexpected.

My day started well. I got up and decided to do some work around the house to keep my mind from spiraling out of control. When these two women showed up, I was smack dab in the middle of cleaning our carpets, my favorite household chore. My carpet was still wet. I sat face to face with two women who would ultimately decide my fate.

I sat in the spot I presume my wife sat and called her into my spirit as I continued the most intense questioning of my life.

"Please state your name for the record."

"Farrell Davis."

The woman with the glasses on the edge of her nose started in. She did not facilitate a smile or any compassion, she fired the barrel, and we were off.

"I'm sure you are aware of what we are dealing with correct."

"Yes, ma'am."

Everything in my spirit was telling me this woman did not deserve my highly respectable "ma'am." However, I was from Alabama, and respect to women and elders was a must. I was raised by my

Grandmother Madear and my mother, she was my rock. Respect for women is all I knew. So, even though I was in my home being investigated, I was who I was, a respectable man.

"So, tell me why would Carli lie about something so serious?"

Her guess was as good as mine, but my guess came with a jail sentence if I didn't answer correctly. I sat back in my chair and began to give them the back story of how we ended up with Carli.

Stopping me before I could fully begin, the lady with the glasses interjected rudely, "We don't need to know all of that."

"With all due respect ma'am, the backstory is necessary. If I can't give the full parameters of what went on, then I can't answer the question."

The state licensing woman shot a look to the other as she turned the volume up on her recorder. She asked me to proceed with what I was saying.

"I would like to hear what you have to say, Mr. Davis. I am the investigating agent, and I do need to hear the backstory."

The woman with the glasses rolled her eyes. I was given free rein to tell the story that led us to this moment. As I came to the end of the backstory portion of the interview process, I looked them both in their eyes and spoke my truth. "I have everything to lose and nothing to gain from this. I—"

Before I could finish my sentence, the evil of the two chimed in adding her two cents to an already aggravated situation.

"What about sexual gratification?"

"Absolutely not! First of all, I love my wife. I have no problems with needing to feel sexually satisfied."

The lead investigator was also taken aback by her partner's comment and continued to jot notes as I spoke. The evil one sat back in her chair, arms folded, unimpressed by my truths.

"Hmm. Would you be willing to submit to a polygraph test?"

Before the words escaped her evil lips, I answered firmly. "Absolutely! I have no problem submitting to a polygraph."

She gave the investigator the side-eye and leaned forward to her note pad. "Hmm. Okay." She said under her breath.

My attention shifted back to the investigator as she was actually speaking to me like I should be spoken to—as an innocent until proven guilty man. Evelina did the exact opposite. I tried so hard to keep my composure. I tried to be still and let God's words move through me because he knew my heart, he knew I would never do this, and he was the only way out of this.

"Have you ever touched Carli inappropriately?"

"NO."

"Have you ever brushed up against her?"

"NO."

"Have you ever accidentally brushed up against her or inappropriately touched her on accident?"

"NO, absolutely not! None of those situations have ever happened at any point in time."

"Okay."

Evelina, now sounding off in a calm and manipulative undertone. "I just want to let you know, Mr. Davis, if there are any untruths uncovered down the line, it is going to be very difficult for you to deal with later. So, you may as well just tell us the full truth now."

"Look, there is not going to be a difference in my story today. There is not going to be a change in my story tomorrow. There is not going to be a change in the story a year from now. The truth is the truth, and nothing is going to change that."

"I see. Well, your wife is the one who is going to have to deal with these things and suffer. You don't want her to put her business in jeopardy. You wouldn't want that, would you? And what about your son?"

"Nothing happened. There's no suffering and nothing to deal with. It didn't happen!"

The investigator continued on with her questions. As uncomfortable as they were, it felt good to answer. I think what hurt the most was that the people Carli told never came to ask me my truth. No one asked me but my wife, my daughters, my son and sister-in-law. My name was being dragged, and no one had the bright idea to just come straight to the source. Today, I was finally able to answer, *on record,* an emphatic 'no' to all accusations brought against my name.

TIFFANY

Every morning since the longest Wednesday ever, I prayed for peace, and for protection over my dad, our home, and our lives. Two investigators showed up today. We were in a tizzy but remained calm while giving them what they needed. They took my mom upstairs first. The look on her face when she came down was the exact look she had when I watched her knees go weak behind Carli's lies. My dad went next. I sat with the daycare kids while my mom stepped outside to breathe before returning to work. My dad came downstairs and entered the daycare, almost lost and slightly angry.

"Hey, Pops. How'd it go?"

"I did not like that."

Our eyes locked, and at that moment, I saw his pain. I saw the suffering of many men whose lives were taken by the games women play when our hearts hurt. Games played simply because they could.

This was not a game. This was really happening, and right now, I was deathly afraid to lose my father. I was afraid to see my mom lose her rock and to lose the only father figure I ever knew. This couldn't be life.

The investigators wanted to speak to me next. However, I had to get to work, so we agreed to talk on the phone later this week. Probably best. Based on how my dad said it went, I knew I did not possess the level of composure they had regarding this. I still wanted to beat Carli's and anyone's ass who came for my father.

I was happy to speak with them because I felt like I had essential information regarding my view of the household. I was in my late twenties, and I came and went within reason. Even though I was part of the family, I took on more of a parent role for my baby cousin and brother. I helped do pickups and drop-offs, observed Carli's behaviors in the house, and maintained a close relationship with her sisters, mostly Brianna. I, too, had text threads highlighting Carli's character and story inconsistencies. So, since I couldn't beat her ass, I channeled energy into my investigative work. I gathered evidence and wrote about what our lives were like in the last five years.

A few days later, I was given my turn in the hot seat. We spoke on the phone that afternoon just before going to work. The lead investigator had been trying to contact me but had a digit off. I eagerly sought her out, ready to tell my story.

"Hi, this is Tiffany."

"Hi Tiffany, this is Dawn, lead investigator on the case against your father, is this a good time to talk?'

"Yes, I've been eager to speak with you."

"Oh, yes? Why is that?"

"Because I feel like I have crucial information to the case that needs to be heard."

"Okay, great. Let's begin. Please state your name for the record."

"Tiffany Raymond."

"Raymond? Your last name isn't Davis?"

"No, when they got married, we just kept mine as my mom's maiden name."

"When they got married? So, Farrell is your stepfather?"

"We don't use those terms, but yes, he is. He came into my life when I was two years old. I'm twenty-eight. I am my mom's child. My sister Iman is his. Together they share my brother, Drew. We are a blended family, always have been."

Silence.

"Where is your father, if you don't mind me asking?"

"He wasn't in my life. Farrell stepped in at two and never left. I love and respect that man like no other," I said while fighting back tears.

"I see, I'm sorry to hear that. How does your father feel about Farrell being in your life?"

"Well, he's dead. He died in 2009. I'm not too sure, nor do I care what he thinks. Next question, please."

"Oh, I'm sorry. Okay. Let's move on. Tell me what happened the day you found out."

"I took my dad to the airport that morning. That afternoon my mom and I were going to workout, but we decided not to. I was in my room on my phone when she ran down. She had this look—this look of the life being drained out of her face. She said Alana just called and said that Carli said Farrell had been molesting her the last five years. I yelled, 'she's lying!' and grabbed my bag to go down to her sister's house. My mom stopped me, and we got on the phone to get to the bottom of it. I spoke with Brianna first, who told me what Carli said. She is saying it happened around eleven PM at night. There was never any penetration that he would rub her body on top of the sheet and call her sexy. Carli said that she threatened to tell, and he started crying. That it started five years ago when she got to the house. I asked Brianna if she believed it. She originally said no then changed her answer to yes because of how she saw Carli react. She encouraged me to look into my dad's eyes to know the truth, I advised her to do the same with Carli. We got off the phone, and the rest of the evening was spent in silence."

"Thank you. Do you believe the accusations?"

"Absolutely not! I live here, and sort of do my own thing, meaning I'm in and out of the house at any and all times of night. My room is on the same floor as Carli's. I often venture upstairs for snacks while talking on the phone to my long-distance boyfriend. That's usually between eleven PM and three AM, our time. I would always find my dad in the same spots, either at the kitchen table on his laptop, in his recliner on his laptop, passed out on the couch snoring, or making a snack—usually popcorn or a bowl of cereal. My boyfriend can attest to this as he witnessed the many late-night conversations me and my dad would have in passing. I say all this to say that I have never seen him going down the stairs passing my living area and into her noisy door—which has a lock—to do all of that then creep back upstairs."

"Her door has a lock on it?"

"Yes, so if she was being harassed in any way, why not lock the door? And because my mom often had to wake her for school, that would've begged the question as to why her door was locked. And ahh freedom from the torment. And her door is loud. Not to mention, her room is a disaster. What she is saying he did virtually impossible without being detected by myself, mom, or brother."

"Okay, I understand you may not have seen anything. However, it does not mean it didn't happen. What if I told you someone saw a butt grab in the kitchen?"

"Well, I'd say you are a liar. No way did that happen in my house, and if it did, why wasn't that part of the original complaint? It seems as if the story continues to change each time she tells it, and her sisters are just eating it up."

"Speaking of her sisters, do you have a good number for them? I haven't been able to reach them."

"I sure do, but you probably won't reach them, they probably don't want to be involved any longer." I gave her their numbers.

"I am trying to help you understand the dynamics in the home and what it's been like. Carli and my brother Drew have been extremely close. I tried to develop a closer relationship with Carli, but I am so much older. The most it's been has been family hangouts, and I've done her hair a few times. Nonetheless, my door has always been open, but she never needed it because she was happy. Every day

I would come home and hear laughter coming from her and my brother. I would hear them joking about stupid Vine videos. She and my sister Iman were thick as thieves. Our family gatherings were amazing. My mom would cook everyone's favorite meal. The twins loved having a family unit and knew Carli was well cared for. My dad has been the man of the family for everyone. He still knocks on any door before entering out of respect for the women in his life. He has never made me or any of my close friends—who also wrote character statements—uncomfortable. He is the most respectable and responsible man—I—I just don't get any of this."

"I understand, but that's not what we are talking about."

"Well, you have to understand the character dynamics of this family and the character of the accused and the alleged victim, right? Carli was a typical teenager. She was dramatic when she was getting in trouble, so the tears she displays is easy for her. She would raise hell every time it was her turn to clean the kitchen. She would go into crying fits, almost paralysis, to get out of being in trouble. We had a meeting about this a few weeks ago, and we sat in her face and asked her to tell us what she needed to reveal, and she said nothing, why is that, Dawn? That was her moment, and she said nothing. Her sisters did the talking for her. She disappeared and came back and let this crap out of her mouth and let her sisters do the rest. As a matter of fact, I have text conversations as proof of what was going on prior to her disappearance. This is a teenager gone rebellious in a major way, and she needed a way out. We became her scapegoat. That's just my two cents, but I understand you have a job to do. I would love to send you the evidence I have. I have a written statement I wrote when we found out, including dates and times of everything. I have a text conversation between me and my Aunt Yolanda, someone who was trolling her via social media, all of which highlight Carli's mental state at the time. I have screenshots of Twitter posts, also highlighting major Jekyll and Hyde behavior. I have all of that ready to send. I feel all of this is crucial to my dad's freedom and needs to be considered. Please, Dawn."

"Okay. Okay. Here's my email. Send me all you have, I want to thank you, Tiffany, for being so honest and authentic. I know this is difficult, and I really wish the best for your family."

"Thank you, Dawn, we are praying the same."

The call ended, and I rushed to send her what I had. She emailed back again, stating that she wished the best for us. That was intense, but I handled myself in a way that I needed to, with power and grace. She was not initially going to consider my evidence, I'm so glad she did, I feel like I made a difference, at least I'm praying so. The rest is left up to God.

MIRABELL

Tiffany did her interview, and I felt confident hearing that Dawn was open to looking at our evidence. Hell, we even provided Carli's boyfriends' information since it also came out later that he knew. Another change in her story. Investigators didn't know she had a boyfriend, we gave them crucial information that should've been provided by the alleged victim. Interesting.

I gave them Yolanda's information since she was in touch with Carli the most. I figured as long as she's honest, investigators would get all the info they needed. Yolanda phoned me that evening to notify me of the investigation. She was frantic and emotional. I let her know that I was indeed aware and that I was the one who gave her information. She said she did not believe it one bit. She even told investigators that her nephew, Farrell, would never do something like this. That he'd been around her girls and that Carli is a liar. She told the truth about her experience in my home. I did not forewarn her of the call because I needed her to be honest, and the element of surprise often blossoms into authentic reactions and responses.

They wanted to go to Drew's school to interview him. As uneasy as it made me, I authorized them to do so because we had nothing to hide. Please interview my son. His honesty and innocence as a child would provide great insight into this as he was closest to Carli.

They came back to my daycare two more times in an attempt to catch me, I guess. Nothing changed. Everything lined up again. During their last visit to my home, they advised me they would be notifying all parents of the children in my daycare. I let them survey the house, her room, they took pictures of the door, the lock, sat on her squeaky bed. Once again, vulnerable, yet willing.

I did my very best with keeping a pleasant poker face. Each morning I greeted each child and wished each mother and father a great day. I secretly hoped they wished me the same, Lord knows I needed it. I tried to put a brave face, but now this situation required a new level of armor. For the most part, working with the kids I cared for had been my escape. The hours of six PM to eleven PM were the hours I essentially *dealt* with the emotions of all of this. Now that they notified parents, it splashed me violently in the face every morning at drop off and every evening at pick up. It invited awkwardly worded texts and calls from concerned parents. It invited awkwardness within me as I struggled to say what's right and what's real. I wasn't ready for any of this yet, somehow the fight in me continued.

The phone calls indeed came in. I lost two children immediately. Their parents came to get them right away. One sighting some excuse. The other no excuse. Both of them did not give notice or honor the terms of our contract— income gone in the blink of an eye. I don't know what we are going to do if I lost any more.

I broke down at the door with the father of two of my long-time children. He asked me straight out. "Hey, Mirabel. We got this call about something that happened with a child. Is everything okay? The wife wants me to ask, I'm sorry."

Tears filled my eyes as I grabbed for the door handle feeling my knees go weak. I spoke from a place of pain. Tears now streaming down my face, I explained to him as much as I could stomach. He empathized with me, said, unfortunately, being a man, you become an easy target. He noted that something similar happened in his family and tore everyone up. Most importantly, he highlighted that we had their support and would not be pulling their kids.

Praise God.

It has been about three weeks since this all went down, and my goodness I don't know how much more I could take. The family on my deceased father's side has really been our strength. They call daily with prayers and spoke through this with Farrell and me. They were supportive in hearing our cries and being what I've been to everyone who had now turned their back on me.

Dear Jehovah

I pray for protection over my business and our finances. I pray that we can sustain ourselves as we continue to trust this process. I am tired, Lord, but I know you want me to fight. I know you put it in my spirit to fight for my truth. I thank you. I thank you for my big heart, even though I've doubted why you gave me such a big heart during this process. I've questioned my very existence during this process. I have been afraid and alone, but today I know you are covering my home, my heart, and my business. If it's meant for the family to recover, I pray we do so gracefully and peacefully so we can make my grandmother proud. Lord, I give it all to you as I rest tonight.

In Jesus' name, we pray. Amen.

Mirabel

TIFFANY

Life had been hell. Danger seemed to lurk behind every corner. I had no one to lean on. I found myself just going into shut down mode and promising to deal with the emotions later. I continued to gather information and watch social media pages as I silently prayed for a miracle, or to at least wake up from this nightmare. I missed my cousins. Although I didn't recognize family anymore, I still missed them and wanted this to be over.

I told my mom that once word got around, we would see who was on our side and who believed the truth. True colors would be seen, and we had to take notice.

Fridays and Saturdays were the only days that life seemed manageable and somewhat normal. I sat in the dark stairway staring at the door that leads to Carli's room. I basked in the soothing sounds of my mother's laughter, something I didn't hear much of anymore. Tonight, as I listen in the stairway, I prayed for my mother's peace through this because although my father's name was being used, this was a clear attack on 'the perfect couple.' She said it herself.

Chapter 22: Social Media Frenzy

TIFFANY

Silence was the best policy, especially after the initial daycare investigation. At least that's what Mom asked of us. So far, no cops had been called, which was weird. Then again, we'd never been through this. How do we gauge how this was even supposed to go?

I had not reached out to Brianna in a few weeks. I blocked them at this point. One: to prevent me from initiating an angry, drunken text exchange. Two: to just block whatever else she may have to say after she said, "I believe Carli."

I'm not upset that they believe her. That is their baby sister, and they handled it as they should have. However, I was upset that they didn't allow the family to meet the way we were supposed to. Otherwise, this would have been shut down. Somehow, I believe Carli knew that and prevented the group meeting on purpose.

This August, I planned to go up North to visit my favorite cousin, Yolanda's daughter, for her birthday. I was reluctant to go as we were under investigation, and I was just too fragile. However, I needed a break, so I went and kept quiet. I tried to enjoy what family I had left. I didn't feel powerful enough to speak about this just yet.

Just a few days into the trip, my mom called saying Carli called my dad. I snuck off to the bathroom to talk, so no one would hear me. My mom revealed that Carli called my dad several times, sounding really weird. She called to speak to him directly. When my mom answered, she said, "this was between me and Farrell."

Once my father got on the phone, she asked him to admit to being a pervert. My father laughed and asked what she was talking about. She expressed that she was in therapy and was advised by her therapist to call him to seek closure. My father responding in kind, "I'm glad you are in therapy because you need it, I don't know what else to tell you."

She then added more to her story, saying he touched her butt and came to her room at night. My father responded the way we all did. "Carli, I couldn't even stomach your room; it stayed filthy. You could barely get in the door. Come on now, Carli!"

After hanging up, my mother called me to say she thought Carli was playing games or she is on something. She said Carli's voice did not sound normal. We all agreed to gear up the fight because this girl was unpredictable.

We continued to stay active with all of them on social media, each of us watching intently at each post, each like, each interaction and engagement. Checking to see if anyone is going to post about it.

I took the lead, I posted an image and quote about forgiveness with a caption speaking directly to Carli. I hoped she would see and feel something and stop this. Hoping to reach them via social media since that was where everyone seemed to focus their energy on. Well, that backfired. My attempt to offer some sort of positive energy to this only provided the perfect pathway for Brianna to say what she's been wanting to say since this all came out.

The public Facebook post hit the airwaves that Thursday evening at six PM. Family near and far were soon made aware of the massive elephant in all of our lives.

BRIANNA: *I am sick of keeping quiet about this. My baby sister suffered for five years at the hands of a monster. Enough is enough. People want to post subliminal messages clearly directed towards my little sister, and I'm sick of it. My sister chose to come forward about something unimaginable and disgusting that she dealt with for five years. She endured suffering that was traumatic at the hands of "family" and was disrespected in the process. There are only two people who know the whole truth that bastard and my sister.*

To the "family" sending shots and subliminal to her and anyone protecting her FUCK YOU, you are disgusting too. I HOPE TO GOD YOUR CHILDREN, SISTERS AND COUSINS NEVER HAVE TO EXPERIENCE WHAT FARRELL DID TO MY SISTER. He is a monster, and if Mirabel wants to protect him, so be it. I hope you are happy sleeping next to a monster.

*So, family, you HAVE **NOTHING** LEFT, and Yes FAMILY, your **PERFECT LITTLE** IMAGE IS RUINED, AND YOU **WILL** LOSE IT ALL IF I HAVE ANYTHING TO DO WITH IT. WHY? BECAUSE YOU ARE CHOOSING TO PROTECT A MONSTER AND TURN YOUR CHEEK TO FAMILY BY NOT CHOOSING HER SIDE, YOU ARE DISGUSTING HUMANS. IF MY FATHER WAS ALIVE, HE WOULD BE AFTER YOU.*

The minutes following the published post, the comments flooded in. Most comments were apologetic for the atrocities Ms. Carli endured. Other comments were full of praise for Brianna protecting her sister. No one really seeing that if this did happen, Brianna just aired her sister's traumas all over social media. Good job, big sis.

When she originally posted it, I was on my way home from work. Part of me wanted to stop in at her place for a little chat. I decided not to. After all, we were way passed a good ole cousin scrapping. She called my father a monster. That cut deep. She aired my mother and father's names on social media. Everything that my parents did for them and Carli over the last five years means nothing at that moment.

When I arrived home, my mom was sitting on the porch, staring off into the distance. She spoke quiet, soft, and direct. "Now, we wait."

"What do you mean, Mom? What do we do? Do we call people? I can't believe she did that!"

"She did that on purpose to get a reaction, we will not react. We will simply wait for our phone to ring and go from there. When the calls come, we will address it and speak our truth, and again we don't know how far this is going, so we have to stay focused."

My mom was always so level headed when it counted. I, on the other hand, was ready to fly off the handle. I'm glad we had each other to balance each other out during this emotional unrest. I didn't like the idea of staying silent, but I also understood that everything was crucial right now. To maintain his freedom, we had to be quiet until the investigation was over.

My mom losing a few kids had been tough on the household, but we'd make it. I stepped up and helped out when I could to prevent any more stress on my poor mother. She looked like she could burst at the seams at any moment. I had to make sure I was there to catch her as everyone had turned their backs on us. At least that's what it felt like. Once this was over, and my father's name was cleared, I knew things would restore. However, right now, our family was being tested.

A few hours went by. The phone never rang. The words Brianna wrote floated along the airwaves piercing themselves in the imprints of every family member present on Facebook. Yet no one called.

Some family members tried to shut it down with Brianna by asking her to remove family business off of Facebook. She angrily declined and kept it up the next few weeks. She was bold. No one could challenge her except me. She would listen to me. Given the circumstances, Brianna was virtually untouchable, and I was practically helpless.

Somewhere in the mix of a real-life investigation and the social media frenzy, more relationships continued to suffer because of a lie that no one initially believed.

Yolanda continued to find amusement in all of it. I know this because that was her exact post. She sat behind her computer "amused" as the family's dirty laundry continued to be aired in the most disrespectful fashion. More deleting and blocking followed.

Since this mess aired onto social media platforms, my mom put a message out to everyone via my dad's social media because she doesn't have a profile. She asked for folks to call her directly and not put her name into anything else. She shut it down, and the phone began to ring.

"Mirabel, it's Yolanda."

"Hi, I'm glad you called. I don't understand why all of this social media bullying is going on, but it has to stop. This is real life happening right now. Come on you guys."

"Mirabel, I know." Yolanda sobbed through the phone. "When the investigator called, I told her Carli is a liar. I did. I told her my nephew, Farrell, would never. I've had my girls around him their whole life."

"Yolanda, I know. Trust me, I do. No one expected this, just say that. This whole social media crap is out of control. We were put in positions where we didn't know what to do. I'm defending my home against the accusations from *family*, someone I took care of. Can you believe that?"

"Me and mine are just staying neutral in all this. It's so sad. Please tell Drew and Farrell I love them. Please, Mirabel. Please tell Farrell I Love *him*."

Her voice trailed off as she got off the phone. My mother's faced looked blank. The first phone call post-investigation seemed to go well. My Aunt said she's neutral. Okay. We could deal with that as long as that meant nothing changed on either side, right? How was any of us supposed to know how to deal with this? After about two months and a clear line being drawn, we're trying to hold on to what little family we could.

My mom was filling us in on the details of the phone call with my Great Aunt Yolanda when her phone rang. It was my Great Aunt Francis.

"Hey, Mirabel. It's Francis! How are you? I just realized I have not talked to you! How are things?"

"Well, Francis, you know we are under investigation. I called you when this all went down. Why haven't you called to see how things were when you said you would be here if needed?"

"Mirabel, I've been busy. Investigation? They called the cops with this?"

"Yes, investigation. So far, it's my home and business. I have never been tested in this way, especially by family."

"Well, Mirabel, you know this family does not know how to love. I found that out a long time ago. I guess now it's your turn to find out, huh?"

"That's unfortunate you feel that way about family, Francis. I know all I've ever done was try to make you feel comfortable and welcome even after you ghosted us after my mom died."

"No, Mirabel, not really. I wasn't even invited to Tiffany's graduation."

"Oh come on, Francis. Now you are just finding stuff to take issue with. What about when we invited you here for Thanksgiving? Farrell and I made you extremely comfortable. You even said it back then. So what are we talking about here? And is this the time family decides to turn on me?"

"You better be careful, Mirabel. You might need one of us to testify."

"You know what, Francis, I *pray* it does not get to that point, and that's it is proven a *lie*. I am keeping everything I have as evidence. I also have Brianna's post. She aired this mess, and I *can't* defend myself because of the investigation. No one is running scared. I have been silenced! I just *can't* believe this, Francis. I have no one. Right now, I just have to take a step back to protect my family against these lies."

"Okay, Mirabel. If that's what you want."

"No, Francis, it's not what I want. It's what I've been forced into."

"Okay, Mirabel. I'll talk to you later."

"Alright. Bye, Francis."

My mom hung up the phone. We sat in silence, wondering exactly what neutral meant. But alas, the first calls were coming in, and the end of this seemed so much closer than before.

MIRABEL

Both of the conversations I had with my aunts were drastically different. I knew it was no coincidence that they called back to back. Nonetheless, I spoke my peace with each of them. It broke my heart to hear my aunt cry. I was just happy that she was honest. I was sorry it hurt her the way it did, but her honesty was everything right now. I wanted to cry with her, but I had to be her shoulder at that moment. She said she would remain neutral and be there for all of her nieces. I get that, just don't let things change for my children and me. As of late, things shifted, but since our talk, she assured me things won't change. We have some support, and we have love. Love is our thing.

My conversation with my Aunt Francis was not shocking at all. She was just pure evil, always has been. Quite narcissistic, but we loved her anyway. Well, we tried to. She revealed that it was my turn to see that the family didn't know how to love. Why in the world would she say such a thing like that? Almost as if she was behind some of this. One could only wonder.

Dear Jehovah

Now that I know where my family stands as far as not believing these lies, I pray that this comes to close soon, Jehovah. I am praying for the strength at this time to endure whatever calls may come. To be strong for my children who are looking to me. I can't crumble even if I want to. God, I pray you keep me lifted in spirit and in grace. This hurts, Jehovah, but I lift it up to you. I know you will heal what needs to be healed, mend what needs to be mended, and clear and what needs to be cleared—Farrell's name included. I pray for my husband, for his strength to hold me up because I know I am leaning so far into him right now. Lord, I pray for the strength of our marriage and pray that Carli reveals this is a lie, that you change her heart and she be forgiven. I pray for forgiveness, Lord.

In Jesus' name, we pray. Amen.

Mirabel

Chapter 23: New York State of Mind

MIRABEL

It had been months of silence from virtually all family. My paternal grandfather in New York was having an eighty-ninth birthday party at the end of this dreary October. Tammy convinced me just to go to get away. Tammy, Tiffany, and I were going to make that trip. We needed it at this point. I couldn't wait to see my grandfather and to be around family. I was so broken but mustered up the energy to be present, laugh, and be surrounded by love—a feeling I missed while going through all of this.

The Raymond side of my family knew what was going on. They didn't believe it either. However, they listened and offered support as soon as they heard the whimper in my voice.

So we went. We flew to New York to celebrate my grandfather's legacy. The pathology and dynamics on my father's side of the family was different. Not to say better or worse, but at this point, I saw things from a different lens—a lens tainted by pain because all I saw here in New York was pure unadulterated love and truth. That's one thing you can't take from my New York family. They keep it real, say what it is or isn't and keep it moving. None of this hush-hush behind the screen interactions.

There was a deep respect for love and tradition. Everyone catered to Grandpa, which was a much different experience than what we had for Grandma in her last years. There was tradition, respect for elders, respect for history, and its preservation. There were in-depth talks.

My Aunt Anita always knew how to get right into my soul with one question, hell one look. Her sincerity was unmatched. Then there was my Aunt Patty, who made the best pork chops, hands down. She tells it like it is. She despised my Aunt Francis because of some old New York childhood drama. Patty had our backs one hundred percent.

Being here, I saw we still had support. That it just might be okay. That our family would restore itself as a family does time and time again.

Coming home, I was excited to see Farrell and to sleep in my own bed again. I was not happy to face whatever this week was going to bring. We'd heard nothing from the daycare licensing investigation. We were on pins and needles, but I determined to enjoy the Sunday evening until we heard something.

As we got home from the airport, Farrell told me that he received a call from a police investigator while we were away. Knots immediately formed in my gut. I sat down because, like before, my knees begin to buckle from under me. Farrell reassured me that he believed that everything was okay. How could he be so sure?

He said the lead investigator on the open case phoned him a few days ago to speak with him to close this case he's had on his desk.

After yet another long hot shower, I made my way downstairs to Tiffany's room to let her know the news.

"They did call the cops."

"Wow, how do you know, Mom?"

"Dad said a detective called him while we were in New York. He wants to meet with him tomorrow to 'close the case,' he says."

"REALLY?! That's good news, right?"

"I hope it is. Since I have to work tomorrow, do you mind going with Dad to meet him? Bring all the evidence you have."

"Of course, Mom. I am ready. The file is ready. We are ready. Do you think he needs a lawyer?"

"No, Dad feels confident that he doesn't need one."

I asked my daughter to go with Farrell for support. She also had a running file of information she'd been gathering. Brianna conveniently deleted her defamation post shortly after I spoke with Francis. We already gathered what we needed, and she better be praying I don't sue for defamation once this was cleared up.

FARELL

Telling my wife the detective called was one of the hardest moments during all of this. After coming home from a trip where she was surrounded by love, I had to be the bearer of bad news. However, I made sure she understood that the detective was extremely lax in his approach, which felt positive. He gave me the option to meet at our home this coming Wednesday. I thought this was a good sign. There didn't seem like there much urgency here, so I would flow with it until we met.

Detective John came that Wednesday evening. Gun on hip, he entered my home, and we sat man to man at my kitchen table. He came in, shook my hand firmly, and placed his file on the table. We sat across from one another at my kitchen table and got right to it.

"Okay, Farrell. Before we begin, I want you to know this is not a formal interrogation. You do not have to answer these questions, and you have the right to a lawyer. I just want to get the formalities out the way." John expressed as he opened the thin file and placed it within my eyes view.

I looked up and told him that a lawyer wouldn't be necessary that I was willing to answer any and all questions he may have.

"Great, so tell me a little about this cheer sport. You guys paid for all of that? I have girls myself let me know what I am in for!"

"Oh, absolutely! We treated Carli just as our own, from gifts to discipline; she was like our child. She wanted to do cheer; we let her do cheer and paid for it all without batting an eye."

"Wow, okay. That probably gets to be expensive. That's great you took her in as your own. Tell me a little about your marriage. Do you and your wife fight? Or often fight to where things get escalated?"

"If you mean do we argue, and our voices tend to elevate, absolutely! What marriage doesn't?"

"Okay, tell me about when your wife went to go stay with your sister-in-law."

"Huh?" Confused, I held my gaze to the detective as I proceeded. "My wife never left this house. And she would never go stay with her sister! If anyone left, it would be me, but no, that never happened."

"Hmm, okay. When I met with Carli, she expressed that this, in fact, happened, and that's when things got worse for her."

"I can emphatically say, neither my wife nor I have ever spent the night away from this house due to a fight or disagreement."

"Okay, now what about Carli walking around the house in sports bras and things of that nature? Is there anything there that you can tell me about how that made you feel?"

"Well, I can tell you that again that didn't happen, not with my wife. My wife wasn't able to walk around like that in the home as a child. She implemented the same for our girls. We are all about being comfortable in the home, but honoring and respecting yourself was the main thing she preached. Carli usually wore those thin strap shirts. Spaghetti straps, I think they call them. And leggings or cheer gear for the most part."

John began jotting down notes on his notepad.

"How is your sex life with your wife?"

Before John could finish, I answered, "no complaints whatsoever, I am a very happy man if you get my drift, John."

We both smiled and proceeded back to business.

"Okay, Farrell. Tell me what you think happened here."

"I really don't know where this all came from. We were getting her ready for graduation and had her all packed up to move her down to her sisters—"

"Was this move planned, or did you guys put her out due to her antics?"

"Absolutely not, that's never been our style. There was a plan that she was on board with and excited about. That was the plan everyone knew would follow graduation. We packed her up and, next thing we know, she doesn't come home, doesn't answer our calls, then this came out."

"Okay, well thank you for being open and honest about all of this, and thank you for meeting me, one last thing before we close this out, can I see the space she lived?"

"Sure thing, follow me."

John got up and followed me downstairs into the garage, where I showed him her room. I showed him her squeaky door, the lock on her door, her squeaky bed. John sat on and took notes. He looked around as I stood in the doorway. As we walked back upstairs, John asked another question.

"So, Farrell, tell me, did you ever go into her room at night?"

"As the man of the house, at times, yes, but only if she left her window open. I would go and close it. Since my daughter also lives on the bottom floor, I checked her area as well. I check and make sure my home is secure like any man would, and let's be honest. I know how these teens get when it comes to sneaking out, so my checking is for safety and to make sure everyone is exactly where they should be."

"Okay. Okay. Makes sense."

"So Farrell, we're going to go ahead and close this case, there isn't enough of anything to move forward, so this is where we meet and part."

John shuffled a few papers and asked if I had any questions.

Wow, just like that, it was over.

I asked John if he minded if I brought my wife and family out to share in the good news. He was more than happy to go over the details with my wife to silence the worry that I felt from her, even if she was in the other room.

MIRABEL

Farrell came into our room where Tiffany, Tammy, and I sat anxiously awaiting our turn for questioning. Tiffany had her laptop and was going over evidence. We sat there for what seemed like hours. It had only been one, but damn, that hour felt like an eternity. Drew was in his room occupied while his father fought for his life. Again, I don't know how we even got here. It was by the grace of God that we arrived at this moment to finally tell our side. I hoped the detective could feel the energy of my home.

"You guys can come out."

We followed a single file down the hallway to greet Detective John, who sat bright-eyed and not at all intimidating. We sat at our dining room table. Farrell sat across from John. I sat next to Farrell. Tiffany sat across from John. Tammy pulled up a chair, and he began.

"Hello ladies, I'm Detective John Johnson. I'd like to start by telling you a little about me. I have been in law enforcement for fifteen years, nine as a detective. Officially I am with the Family Protection and Child Exploitation Unit. I am also a member of the FBI's Child Exploitation Task Force, and a member of the ICAC, the Internet Crimes Against Children the last six years. I've completed over one thousand hours in ongoing training and education relating to interview techniques, interrogation, and child exploitation. I say all of this to say that I'd like to think of myself as a human lie detector, meaning I have a solid understanding of human behaviors and efforts behind self-preservation. I have studied my craft and poured into it with the same efforts I would expect someone to if my daughters needed it. You all need to know how serious I take my job and how serious I am about protecting this community, our community."

We all sat there, glazed over. Farrell seems more at ease than I expected. Tiffany looked scared. Tammy's face was blank. I just sat there unsure of what this man is about to say.

John continued. "After conducting a few interviews and meeting with the alleged victim, I can't say that I feel confident moving forward with any charges. Even after meeting with Farrell, I still don't have enough to move forward in any manner besides closing the case out."

A silent sigh of relief emerged from our bellies. Unbeknownst to me, tears filled my eyes and dropped silently as the last four months crept to a halt. Farrell wiped my tear and smiled at John, asking him to proceed.

"From our phone call, the interview just now, and from the investigation I conducted the last few months, I can see that your husband is a standup guy. Your home is beautiful and warm. From what he was telling me, it's unfortunate that this has happened to your family, it seems like you all were very close."

"We were that's why this was so bizarre" tears going full force now.

"Well, I can share with you that I met with Carli one time. The other attempts I made were ignored. We met for about two hours and, well, I can tell she is troubled. For the lack of a better word. I let her know that she can bring her own appointed advocate for emotional support given the nature of the initial report; however, she presented alone. I wasn't able to meet with or even get ahold of her sisters. They, too, did not answer the calls I put out to them. It's also clear that her story has changed several times, given the nature of my interview with Farrell and the evidence that matches up with what you all have presented. She presented unemotional and very matter of fact, which is neither here nor there in regards to the investigation. I even tried calling her last week to let her know we don't have anything to go on. I have yet to get a callback. So, that brings us to this moment. How it works is when the initial report is taken, it is our job to refrain from any judgment. We have to really consider each case at face value and virtually unpack it to find the good stuff we need to move forward with filing charges. Once the patrol unit takes the initial report, it is funneled to someone like me to follow up with and formulate the investigative plan, and this means conducting interviews. We begin with hosting what we call "controlled calls," where we get the alleged victim and alleged accuser on a call together and try to get something from that. All interviews need to be as thorough as possible. This case was no different. I give every case the same amount of effort and attention, which has been a critical catalyst for our one hundred percent conviction rate."

Farrell stroked the small of my back while I searched for something, anything to say. I couldn't. The last four months had been hell. Beyond hell, if I must say. Between the daycare licensing pop-ups and the fear of the unknown, I had to take a minute to take it all in. My man was safe, our home is protected, and we are *finally* free from this.

"Thank you, John, for doing such amazing work. You have no idea the turmoil we've all had to go through" Tiffany mustered up the very words I had trouble speaking. She was always so good with her words. "Our lives have been turned upside down, and no one cared. After Brianna posted her nasty Facebook post, the entire family went silent."

"Facebook post?" John asked.

Tammy, shuffling through the evidence file she collected, found Brianna's post and handed it over to John as he jotted her name down on his pad of paper.

"This was posted two months ago? While I was conducting my investigation? Hmm"

"Yes, it was, and we could do nothing about it but sit and wait for calls that never came. We couldn't respond or defend ourselves because, at the time, we only knew about the daycare licensing investigation."

"Interesting," John said in an almost disgusted fashion.

"I will say that I hope that God restores your family in the fashion that best suits all of you, I have a strong faith and know that only he can restore things of this nature, believe that."

John sat and talked with us for another hour or so. His dispatch phoned just to make sure he was okay, and he was. He sat comfortable and in control. He allowed us to ask questions, and for once in the past four months, we all felt normal again, even if it was only for two hours.

Farrell walked John downstairs and out to his car. When he returned, we brought Drew out of his room and hugged him, letting him know his dad was okay. We phoned our few supporters and shouted to them on speakerphone, "CASE CLOSED!" We hugged, we cried, we took a shot, we laughed, we cried some more, and we were all finally able to rest that night with a settled mind and clear heart.

My current reality was that my husband was safe. My home was warm enough to make a cop feel comfortable. I was somewhat put together with the strength of someone's prayer.

That night, I laid in my husband's arms and listened to him snore as we drifted off to sleep; it was the most beautiful and soothing sound that I ever did hear.

Dear Jehovah,
THANK YOU.
Your faithful servant,
Mirabel.

CHAPTER 24: A Quiet Christmas

MIRABEL

Just one week after John left our home, life seemed to settle a bit more. We had a little powwow when he left. We knew our phones would be ringing. Everyone would know that this was a big mess, and we'd move forward as a family.

Daycare licensing came knocking once again. Once again, my heart fluttered with anxiety, unsure of what they would say this time. Licensing informed me that my business was indeed safe and sound. Praise God. They instructed me to continue doing what I was doing because they, too, found nothing remotely close to giving them the right to shut me down. They spoke with the children I cared for and their parents and came into my home unannounced several times and found nothing each time.

Unfortunately, this occurrence left me with an inquiry in the daycare licensing system. That meant potential clients could see there was a complaint made, and I was left to explain should they ask. I was angry because I'd been in business for fifteen years and never had a complaint, and now this. Proper perspective reminded me to be grateful that I still had a business to run and that our family was no longer under a magnifying glass.

Once the case was closed with the local police department and with daycare licensing, we knew the calls would come. We knew our family was going to inquire about the results. We knew that although it was going to be awkward for all of us, that we would eventually pull together and hash this out, at least that's what we all hoped.

Fast forward to December, one-month post clearing, and our phones remained silent. Yolanda hated me for some reason. At least that was the word she put out to the family. I couldn't for the life of me understand why she felt that way when our last conversation was peaceful. She cried to me, expressing the hurt we all felt. She said she loved us and would be here. Now, not only did she hate me, but it seemed as if she was trying to get everyone else to hate me.

This situation went on far too long. Everyone only communicated through subliminal social media posts. The ones who said they were neutral and would be here for us in the situation ended up hating us. All we did was defend the truth, and we are being hated, ridiculed, ignored, and disrespected in the process.

Our annual cousins' Christmas was uneventful this year. It was just us, which was perfect, just quiet. The usual holiday cheer that danced the halls of my home was gone. What we were left with were a family of five who stood grounded in the truth, fought for it, showed up for it, got beaten down for it, cried for it, and became hated for defending it. We were martyrs of the truth. We fought relentlessly for Farell's freedom—for our freedom. So, if we had to spend a Christmas reflecting on that, then so be it.

It was hard to watch my children. Tiffany put on a brave face because she fully understood what happened. However, there was an underlying sadness present for not being with her cousins, not hosting the event, and not winning the gingerbread house contest. Loyalty was everything to my girl Tiff. Drew, who was much younger, was aware of the nature of what Carli did. I saw him trying to be happy while constantly looking to his dad and me for comfort or asking if we were okay. I lied to him at least once.

As this tumultuous year finally came to a close, I prayed for the safety of my family into this next year. Tiffany would be moving across the country. Our dynamics had already shifted drastically. I had no idea what the next year would bring. I just knew I couldn't take another year like the last.

So, we had our quiet Christmas and played our old school holiday music. Tammy whipped up the Christmas inspired drinks, Farell played the music. Tiffany and I danced around, trying to make it feel somewhat like it used to, forgetting that it is exactly how it should be. I cooked a beautiful Christmas Eve dinner that year. Getting in my kitchen to feed my family was my therapy. I went to town and made everything I could to show them the extent of my love. That Christmas, we had a feast for the fighters in my life, their silent chews and clean plates were the *only* gifts I needed that year.

Dear Jehovah,

I come to you with an open heart this Christmas evening and I ask that you help me to understand the depths of all of this. I will not ask why this happened because I know you are an awesome God, and you don't put your children through things like that without purpose. I ask that you help me to see my purpose in all of this.

Taking Carli in, I was honoring my aunt's wishes. I will continue to pray for Carli's safety and her heart. I pray that we can move forward and heal as a unit if that's what's in your will.

I don't know where to go in this next year. I just know I need you with me. Lord, you give me strength in ways I haven't been able to duplicate on my own. Thank you for saving us Jehovah. For protecting Farrell and allowing us to be strong enough to fight. Thank you.

I ask that in this next year, we see the beauty of your love and the beauty restored within our family. I ask that you help me not to internalize any of their hate as anything more than just being hurt. Help me to see the vision you have for my life and my family because, right now, we are lost. Stay with us even in the aftermath of all of this and guide us along the way. I don't know what will come of my family, of Carli, or any of them. Still, I continue to pray for their protection as well, their safety and their hearts. I trust and believe that no man can bring this back together, it has to be you, and when you do, we'll know if that's what's in your will.

In Jesus' name, we pray. Amen.

Mirabel

Chapter 25: Spiritually Solid

TIFFANY

It had been five years since the incident when I've moved back home. I'd successfully built a brand that allowed me to venture home where there was comfort and love. I'd experienced a lot of loss in these last five years. I had no cousins to call on. I didn't have aunts I could call if my mom was difficult. I didn't have uncles to protect me if the world seemed a bit scary. I only had my mother, father, aunt, brother, and sister. That's it. That was all I really needed—all I'd been accustomed to needing when everyone else turned their backs.

My cousins were my first best friends. We bonded in a way that almost made us like sisters, especially me and Brianna. There was a closeness there that each of us understood and catered to because we knew each other's struggle. We'd been there for each other during some crazy family times. She held my hand at my grandmother's funeral and made sure I was okay. That memory stayed with me.

I was the oldest of all the female grandchildren. I was a fourth-generation daughter and a direct descendant of my Great Grandmother Bella. Her heart was manifested within me. I also held the strength of the grandmother and will power of my mother through my veins. However, I was lost in this situation. I internalized it all, believing that I never mattered to any of them. I felt used, like the last twenty-eight years was nothing but me showing up and them taking.

My mind ran in circles trying to understand why humans couldn't just say "sorry" and genuinely mean it. I couldn't understand why social media was the go-to when we all lived in the same city. Hell, I fell into it too. I internalized everything and tried to hold on to what little family was left as best I could. That was until I was told we made things awkward because we stood by the truth.

I was disgusted by every single person on that side of my family. I prayed for their hearts to change for the greater good the community they each served because, as we've seen here, hurt people hurt people.

I didn't know if we would ever be right again. We were so far left. How could we? At this point, life had to go on without them. I understood what my soul wanted and needed; that low vibrational energy was not it.

Not one person stood up for me the way I'd stood up for them. Not one person held us in high regard or was loyal to the cause. Not one person was genuine in their attempts to connect during this time; it was all a funnel for information. Family members came to hang out with us, pretending like they were building with us but then go over to their side to hate us. Who asked anyone to pick a side anyways? This went deeper than choosing sides. There were hate posts displayed all over social media. Fake attempts at family gatherings where only some family was included just to throw it in our face. There has been manipulation of relationships. Many relationships ended because people were too afraid to stand with what was real and to speak their truth.

I was serious when I told my cousin Brianna that I would ride this wave with my dad until it's over. Now that it was over, I was still riding the wave of truth. However, I no longer internalize their inconsistencies as a family as my own. I did not reach out to anyone because I was too angry, besides they were all blocked on my phone. That's how I deal with this type of disloyal shit. Block it and move on before I catch a case.

I had no intention of reaching out, but I felt there needed to be a conversation at some point. When my anger subsides, and I can face Alana, Brianna, and Carli, I would with God's grace. The original people involved needed to have a conversation first. If that couldn't happen, then everything would stay as is.

At this time in my life, I'd had grown tremendously as a woman. This growth came at the cost of being stripped away from everything I knew, loved, and appreciated about life and family. I prayed and fought to be the person I was today, and I was not going back.

One of the great leaders and wise men beyond his years, Malcolm X stated, "A man who stands for nothing will fall for anything."

I was proud to say that I stood firm in the truth. I stood firm in remaining loyal to the cause. I stood firm in being cooperative during the investigation. I stood firm in not beating Carli's ass like a good big cousin should. I stood firm in asking God how I could grow from this and not grow cold in my heart. I stood firm in the fight of my life, and the fight for my father. I gladly stood on the front line with him because I knew him and knew he would do the same for me.

I had to learn inner strength by choosing to be still when rage came to the forefront upon Brianna's post. I had to understand that healing was subjective, and everyone was on their own journey. I had to learn that hate was negative energy and was far more powerful than positive energy, as long as the intent was evil. I had to learn to silence the hatred of the words spoken about my mother from people she cared for deeply. I had to learn to respond rather than react, especially with the initial news. I had to learn to think before I speak. I had to learn to let go of people and things that did not serve me. I had to learn what served me because what served me five years ago was amazing and beautiful and complete, and today that is not the case. I had to discover God. I had to trust in him and put full faith that this will work out. I had to study the word every single day, practice the word and repent at the end of the day when I fell short, which was often. I had impure thoughts of my family and was uncomfortable knowing I gave them so much of me only to be used and discarded. I had in-depth conversations with family members that made me believe they had my back during this time. Long lost cousins who swooped in only to take my vulnerability, run with it and capitalize on it for selfish gain.

What about me, my brother and sister? Who do we go to if our parents left this earth? We had none of them but gained so many other valuable entities that I knew God has sent directly to us.

Maybe it's in his will that we never reconnect. I'm not exactly sure, but I knew this would not be in vain. I guess if I had to learn all of this through cousins and family, then it was worth it because the person I am today can't be rocked in any way, shape, or form.

I forgave Carli a long time ago, I knew she didn't fully understand the extent of what she did. I believe she just wanted to keep her sisters away from us as their punishment. While keeping us apart from the entire family because, once again, hurt people hurt people.

Initially, she said she did not want to go to the cops, yet after our sit-down, she went and twisted her story several times. Her reasoning behind hiding this for five years was because she said she did not want to break up the family and then proceeded to do precisely that. She also said she didn't want to mess up the perfect couple, which she did not, and that's why we are blessed.

Two years after the initial allegation, Carli got herself into more trouble. Voices chattered around the family, and the news made its way to us. She ended up living with our Uncle Ernest, who was very close to her mother and best friends with her deceased father. She took shelter with him temporarily because no one else wanted to deal with her. It seems as if everyone was afraid to interact with Carli because we had just scratched the surface of her manipulative capabilities.

While in his care, Uncle Ernest flat out asked her what the hell happened.

"Carli, what happened? You know if something like this happened, you could have called me. I would have handled it. So tell me what the hell happened."

Shocked at his directness yet quickly avoiding any further details regarding the incident, Carli replied, "I was just mad at Mirabel." Then she retreated to her room.

"WHAT THE FUCK, CARLI!" Uncle Ernest stepped out onto his porch, dropped his head in his hands, and cried.

The destruction of the family took its toll on our usually jovial and sometimes annoying Uncle. After our matriarch, Grandma Bella, passed, he lost his family too. Weekly visitors that would pop in to check in on him and Grandma stopped once she passed. Once these allegations came out, the family gatherings went from bountiful to non-existent as the telephone game led us further into the extinction of Grandma Bella's legacy.

A week after her revelation, Carli stole two hundred dollars from Uncle Ernest and left his home in the middle of the night to go live with a friend a few hours away.

As time went by, I had to forgive her because it felt better in my spirit to know that she was young, hurting, and afraid. Instead of believing that she was plotting this all along. It felt better to know that I have the power to heal through forgiveness and understand that everything happened for a reason, that reason hadn't come to fruition yet, but I was hopeful.

Today, five years later, we sat in a better mental space. We'd fully adjusted to these new dynamics in what's left of my great grandmother's family. I can honestly say the family was no longer bothersome to hear or speak about because we could now laugh at the good old times. Prior to this moment, hearing about them facilitated a rage in me that I could not control most times. It hurt in the deepest parts of me to see all the cousins getting together, and my siblings and I not even be considered. I had to reframe my pain to fit into the reality I wanted to see and feel. My dad was safe, our home was protected, and healing from this trauma was necessary.

I knew we are missed by them, just not enough to pick up the phone and stop it. We'd also accepted this reality and remained open to a conversation. Until then, we sat divided and conquered by the woes of a wounded teen.

Dear Jehovah,

I want my family back. I want us to heal. I want us to acknowledge and respect each other's pains and support each other through the healing.

If it is in your will, God, I ask that you show me how to proceed with grace and humility. Help me to release the anger I had associated with Carli and her lies and the people who didn't stand up for us when they knew the truth. Please stay with me during this time, God. Soften my heart and allow me to turn the trauma into a teachable moment in forgiveness. Thank you.

In Jesus' name, we pray. Amen.

Tiffany

Chapter 26: Bella's Eye View

BELLA MARIE

Dear family,
Bella Marie here, the matriarch of the family. I see what is going on down there, and I am disgusted with every single one of you. You allowed one person to tell a lie that destroyed the very legacy I created singlehandedly. I had ten children and took all ten of you to California for a better life. I exposed you all early to the fantastic works of our Jehovah God. He has blessed us tremendously.

We have always been able to bounce back from family issues, bigger issues if I might add. This should not have been any different. My heart hurts watching all of you feud in such ugly ways. The hate that is coming out is a clear indicator that Satan has his hand all over my family. My heart breaks as I sit in silence, wondering where I went wrong. My presence was your protection, and now that I have passed on, it is up to you all to tap into what you know to be true about the God I taught you all to serve.

To my eldest grandchild, Mirabel, you are the one who took care of me in my last days, who took care of your mother in her final days, who took care of Cara in her last days, and who took on Cara's children. I am sorry I have left you with such evil spirits. Had I been there when this accusation came about, none of this would have happened.

I was our peacemaker, and I passed my torch to you without hesitation. You are the one who has been around everyone, stayed mentally sane, and grew from your experiences in a beautiful and godly way. I know you are not perfect, Mirabel, but you have a spirit in you that is strong. You are a force to be reckoned with. I'm sorry the family turned their backs on you and your family.

To the children of my beloved daughter Cara—Alana, Brianna, and Carli—I am disappointed in you for not trusting what you know and believe versus what you hear. I know you had a responsibility to your sister to protect her. Without much guidance, you did what you had to do to help her. I am sorry you didn't have anyone in your corner to guide you through this. I am also sorry that you felt it was the right move to post our family business in full detail online. Everyone's role was significant. Your role was crucial in stopping this from going on as long as it did, had you followed through. I know you did not know how to handle this. I'm sorry I was not there to guide you in a more forgiving direction. The hate you displayed for your cousins is shocking as I remember you all being so close.

You were not guided by anyone that was not led by selfish hidden agendas. People got close to you guys under false pretense, and I know you suffered greatly, I see it written all over your faces. You just wanted that sense of family. You were surrounded by many but never felt heard. Mostly props in a picture for a few likes and a couple shares.

Carli, you know you had a beautiful life with Mirabel and Farrell. We all knew it. We all felt it. It showed in your smile when you would come to see me. It showed in how excited you were to be able to participate in regular teen things. It proved to all of us that you were okay and that you were thriving in life. We all knew you would dance your way into whatever college you wanted because you were that good at pouring into your craft.

To my eldest children, you should be ashamed. To turn your back on family in the manner that you did, and the successful attempts you had at turning others against each other is sickening. I've watched from a bird's eye view the destruction of one lie tear my entire family down, and no one has it in them to fix this. I taught you to know our God, so why do you restrict yourselves from hearing the truth of what he wants for your life?

My children, rebuke the Devil and his wicked ways and heal. Why are you wavering to the ways of the world? Maybe I did raise you this way. Perhaps the influence I had on my grandchildren and great-grandchildren was the love you all sought. However, I did my best and had peace with the fact that I was a single parent of ten, and you all survived. I am sorry for the hurt I caused any of you, and I understand that this may be my payback into eternity.

My legacy, my spirit, and the love I exuded are being lost as the years go on. The more hate that is being spewed surrounding this, the more taxing it will be to find common ground.

I am here, in heaven, with Cara, who is unable to speak on how sorry she is for the hurt caused by her children. Sharon is here too, disappointed yet fighting, protecting and guiding her girls as they adjust to life without the family unit we all knew and loved.

Laughter was our thing. Family dinners in my tiny well-designed apartment was our thing. Games of Canasta was our thing. Dancing was our thing. Jokes were our thing. We were a family of a twisted kind of love and twisted humor that worked for us.

With that, we have been able to get through anything. My absence proves that you will need greater strength for the fight ahead, so I call you to do the work.

Sit down, have a one-on-one conversation to unpack every bit of this. Sit with every emotion, listen to every word, find the actual truth, and heal in a grand way. I encourage each of you to apologize for your role; you all had one. Trust me, I know. I watched it all. Frankly, each one of you who didn't attempt to stop the nonsense is responsible. Each one of you that saw negative posts and didn't call is responsible. Those of you that remained neutral and flip-flopped every year are responsible. Those of you that used this as an opportunity to get close to Cara's girls for selfish reasons are responsible. Those of you that never believed it from the beginning yet didn't join in Mirabel's fight is responsible. Those of you that didn't have the balls enough to stand up to what was right and true are responsible. We are a family, and this affected every single one of you on a deeper level. We are only as strong as our weakest link, and Carli is ours, and you all failed miserably.

The disrespect was loud; make the healing and apologies louder. Be bold like I taught you. Be assertive like a taught you. Show the world that no lie is greater than the force of pure unadulterated love. Show them that healing is our thing.

Make it right.

Your mother, grandmother, and great grandmother,
Bella Marie

About the Author

"Write what hurts and watch it heal." That is the mantra that has empowered the imagination and willpower to tell this story for upcoming Author, TK Ray. Using colourful language and descriptive tone, Tk's imagination provides a safe space to unpack a beautiful and twisted tale inspired by true stories of real family dynamics that everyone can relate to.

TK Ray was born in San Diego, California to a fifteen-year-old mother and fourteen-year-old father in the late eighties. Born to two young teens, TK found herself tainted by the statistics of becoming a teen mother herself. She found solace in the world of literature as her own private journals became her voice when shyness took over. She began to understand the world in more intuitive way and birthed that intuition into an imagination that has fuelled much of her writing. Much of her writing is personal however as the years have gone by, have included poetry, music, obituaries, blog posts and now expanding into the genre of fictional literature.

TK is a certified Holistic Health Practitioner and practicing in southern California. She fuses her knowledge in holistic health with that of her knowledge of her bachelor's degree in health science to better serve her community in wellness and education. Her wellness blog embodies all of who she is as she has expanded on her writing style to help others follow their passion, peace, and purpose. Tk's writing style is sure to leave you on the edge of your seat as she paints a portrait of pain drawn out by the light in her own fighting spirt.

Acknowledgements

Thank you to God for allowing me to be a vessel for HIS story he wants the world to hear.

Thank you to my family, the fighters, we did it. Thank you for the encouragement on the tough writing days.

To my siblings, niece and nephews, we stay winning. Period.

Thank you, Aunt C, for encouraging me to write, encouraging my vision and creativity. Thank you for visiting me in Atlanta.

Thank you to John and Disha for providing my safe haven.

Thank you to my Truth Tribe (JTZMC) for letting me write when I needed to, thank you for listening to chapters, providing feedback and loving me through the writing process.

Thank you to my mentor and Coach D in Atlanta thank you for your energy of love and commitment to make sure I reach my fullest potential.

To my dad, thank you for the purest most genuine love I could've ever asked for.